thorns

Other books by Kate Avery Ellison

The Curse Girl

Once Upon a Beanstalk

Frost (The Frost Chronicles #)

thorns

Kate Avery Ellison

For my Mom

THORNS: THE FROST CHRONICLES #2

Lia Weaver went against everything she'd ever known when she risked her life to help a Farther fugitive named Gabe escape from the Aeralian soldiers, and her life changed forever. And the Frost changed, too—the Farthers have taken over her village, a new group of vigilantes calling themselves the Blackcoats are making plans to overthrow the Farther occupiers, and the Thorns are seeking for her to join them.

Lia seeks to fight back against the evil and injustice that has swallowed up her home, but danger lurks at every turn. The monsters that dwell in the deepest regions of the Frost are growing bolder and more dangerous every day, a Farther noble takes up residence in the village on a mysterious mission, and Lia discovers even more secrets embedded in her past.

As the frozen world of the Frost grows even more perilous, can Lia survive?

ONE

I STOOD ALONE in the middle of the farmyard, the wind tugging at my hair and stinging my chapped lips as I faced the tree line. The sun had barely risen, and the shadows made a dark smudge against the edge of the farm's fields. I stared at the place where the blue-tinged darkness touched the pristine white of the freshly fallen snow and felt a flood of apprehension rush through my veins.

Those shadows were a line of demarcation, a warning, an invisible sign shouting to me to stay out, because beyond them was the Frost, and it was not safe there.

It was early morning, and the sunlight was hidden behind a thick swath of storm clouds. But enough light permeated the frosty air to illuminate the yard of my family's sad little farm. To my right, the barn hunkered down against the wind like a bony cow with her back half-covered in ice from the night before. The horse paddock straggled behind it in a lopsided circle. Several of the fence posts were bound with rope to keep them from sagging. Ice covered everything in a slick, sinister shine.

The farmhouse was to my back, comforting and solid despite the fact that it looked ready to topple over. The whitewashed boards blended with the snow, white on dirty white, as if the house were hiding. The windows were dark. My brother and sister still slept. There was no use rising before dawn, for no one went out while it was still dark. Our frozen world was always perilous enough with its population of bears, snow panthers, and mothkats. But after dark the most dangerous monsters in the Frost roamed.

Watchers.

I scoured the wall of forest for any glimmer of red light that would betray a Watcher's gaze. I strained for the sound of shrieking they sometimes produced, but the only thing I heard was the whisper of wind against the Watcher Ward that hung over our door. The bits of wood and bone clattered together. They were painted blue and carved like snow blossoms, the only things that turned the Watchers away.

I tugged my cloak around me as my blood sang with unease.

Every time I set foot in the Frost it reminded me of a night two months ago. The night Adam Brewer and I helped a Farther fugitive named Gabe escape. The night I realized that I was not the same person I used to be. Now, just thinking about Gabe sent a dagger of pain through my chest.

A grim hush wrapped around me as I stepped through the dark barrier of limbs and into the forest. The trees were slashes of black against the white; the snowflakes that drifted down were specks of softness against my cheeks and lashes. The air throbbed with silence except for the hiss of my breath escaping from my teeth and the wet squish of my boots against the icy roots beneath my feet. My heart pounded against my ribs, but I kept going. I was not some fragile, made-of-glass village girl. I was a Weaver. I lived far from the walls that protected most of the Frost dwellers.

I had no choice but to be brave.

A branch snapped in the distance. I pressed myself again a tree, the rough bark scratching my palms as I flattened against it. My hands found the knife at my belt.

A white doe bounded from a thicket and darted past me, her ears flickering back to catch the sound of my sigh.

Not a snow panther. Not a bear.

Not a Watcher.

I pressed on, but the back of my neck prickled with apprehension with every step. I felt as if a hundred unseen eyes watched from the shadows. Memories swept over me again. The red glow. The guttural growls. The swift slice of claws as they dug into the snow.

In theory, the forest was safe from the Watchers during the light of day. They only came out once the shadows had pooled together and the moon had risen, the time when we huddled close to our hearths and burned our fires high. I could even make the trek to the secret place deep in the Frost where we'd taken Gabe, the place where the mysterious gate that had swept him away from me stood waiting.

But I refused to finish that thought. Gabe was gone. I had to focus on survival now.

Bat-like scavenging creatures called mothkats were already hovering over the trap. Their bright, beady eyes focused on me, and they fluttered away as I approached. I waved my arms, and they took to the sky. Disgusting vermin.

11

Mothkats weren't dangerous individually, but a large enough pack of them could descend and strip flesh with their sharp little teeth and claws. They were just another perilous aspect of the Frost.

I crouched and looked at the trap.

A dead animal dangled between the metal jaws. A white rabbit with gray little paws. Ivy would be heartbroken if she saw it.

I lifted the body out, placed it in my sack, and carefully reset the contraption. As a little girl, I'd sometimes gone out into the forest with my Da to set traps when our food supplies dwindled and we were still days from turning in our quota and getting fresh food from the village. Now, I was doing it alone.

The rabbit was mostly fur and bones, proof of the long, hard winter. It wouldn't be enough to feed us until quota day. I bit my lip and gave one last glance to the woods before turning to head home.

I ran the whole way back. The rabbit flopped against me. The cold air burned my nostrils and made my cheeks sting. Snow swirled around me, kicked up by my boots and knocked loose from my passage through low-hanging branches.

Panting, I reached the farmhouse. A mothkat cry split the air somewhere far above me. The Watcher Ward clattered and spun in the wind. The wind whispered faintly over the snow. It was all Frost music—wild and uncertain and weirdly beautiful in a way that made my chest ache.

I paused to knock the snow from my shoes before opening the door and stepping inside.

The warmth of the house curled around me, thawing my frozen cheeks and lips. I threw off my dripping cloak and crossed the main room to the fireplace. I laid down my bag with the rabbit and stoked the glowing coals into feeble flames. My numb fingers were clumsy with the kindling. When the fire burned bright again, I pulled out my hunting knife and set to work on the rabbit.

"Lia?"

My twin brother Jonn's voice was just a whisper behind me. I turned.

He leaned against the doorframe of the lower bedroom, the one my parents had used, the crutches under his arms holding him up. We were twins, almost identical, although I'd always teased that he was the prettier one. His eyes were too large for his thin face, framed by thick lashes, and I could see veins in his hands and beneath his eyes. He looked at the rabbit and then at the water clock over the mantel.

"Just checking the traps," I said.

My gaze dropped to his left leg and slid away. The limb was thin and twisted beneath the fabric of his pants, and the bare foot that poked out shone with scar tissue. We were twins—he was the same age as me, old enough to be a man, but he hadn't been able to walk properly since he was just a small child, so he'd never received an assignment or permission from the Elders to start a family. The accident that had rendered him a cripple in the eyes of the village had given him frequent seizures and sick spells, too. He could hobble around on crutches, but the effort it took exhausted him. He rarely left the house. He hadn't been to the village since my parents' deaths. My father had carried him on festival days and for some of the Assemblies, but there was no one to do that now, and besides, I knew the looks of pity and disgust the others gave him hurt.

"Are we that low on food?"

"We're always that low these days," I muttered.

13

He looked like he might say something, but thought better of it. Instead, he hobbled to his chair by the fire and lowered himself slowly into it. The crutches fell to the floor with a thump, and he reached for the basket of yarn at his feet. Quota day was coming, and we weren't finished with the yarn and thread we owed the village Elders in exchange for the grain, salt, and other supplies that kept us from starvation during the winter months. Idle hands were a luxury none of us could afford.

I finished skinning the rabbit and put the meat in a pot to stew over the fire before cleaning up and sinking into the chair opposite him. The threadbare cushion poked at the backs of my knees where the feathers were beginning to push through the fabric. I shifted, reaching for a tangle of yarn to roll as well. The fire crackled and snapped on the hearth, and the wind whispered at the windows and sighed in the cracks. The room smelled of smoke, wet wool, and dust.

"What were you doing out so early?" he asked. "You usually check the traps after breakfast."

Words crowded my mouth and lay heavy on my tongue, excuses mostly. I didn't want to talk about the burning ache that kept me from sleeping and drew me to the edge of the forest. I didn't want to involve him in anything having to do with the Thorns, or the Farthers. It was too dangerous. This was my burden, mine alone. I just shook my head. "I couldn't sleep."

Jonn's voice was low, raw. "He's not coming back, Lia."

I flinched. He meant Gabe.

Gabe had been on the run, halfway to somewhere else, on a journey out of here. We'd done everything to see him on his way, and I'd come to care about him, and now he was gone...

And I was left holding myself together in his wake. Just like I always did when somebody left. You'd think I'd have learned by now not to care about people, because you just couldn't count on them to stick around.

My brother watched my face, and I could tell he was looking for hints of emotional distress. But if he expected me to shatter like fine china, he was mistaken. I was carved from the Frost. I was a Weaver's daughter. I was ice and wood and frozen rain.

I cleared my throat. "If you think I'm going to fall apart missing him, you're wrong," I said. "I don't pine for people. There's too much on the line to be moping around or feeling sorry for myself."

Jonn was silent. I felt his disbelief in his lack of comment.

"I'm not like that," I said, frustration creeping up my throat, tasting like bile. "I've never been like that. He's gone. It's done. Let's pick up the pieces of our lives and move forward just like we always do. There's a lot more to worry about than silly emotional attachments."

"Silly emotional attachments," he repeated. His eyes dropped to my wrist where I wore the scrap of leather that I'd found marking Gabe's place in the book he'd been reading before he left us. I'd been wearing it ever since the night Gabe left us.

"What else would you call it?" But I disagreed with myself even as I spoke the words. I pushed my sleeve down so it covered the bracelet.

I glared at him until he lowered his head and tangled his fingers in the yarn. The backs of my eyes burned, and my throat squeezed painfully tight. I wasn't sure if it was the subject matter or Jonn's dogged persistence in dealing with my emotions that triggered these almost-tears, but either way, it had to stop.

15

The silence got too thick, and it made me jumpy. I stood.

"I should see to the animals. And after that, I have to go into the village. We're nearly out of food, and we need something more than that scrap of rabbit to feed us until quota day. Unless you'd rather eat nothing but dried turnips and potatoes?"

"Lia—"

"I'm fine," I said, gritting my teeth. "Really."

He sighed and let me change the subject. "Fish would be good. Just be careful. You're in a mood today. Don't rile the Farthers."

I wasn't in a "mood." I was sick of being harassed. But all I said was, "I'm used to the Farthers by now."

Farthers. Saying it felt like cursing.

"I'm going to milk the cow and collect the eggs. You should make sure Ivy gets up. That yarn has to be finished—quota is due in two days."

I felt his gaze on my back the whole way to the door. I dragged on my cloak, wrenched the door open, and stamped back out into the yard.

I let the wind sting my eyes until they streamed water.

~

Ivy was up when I returned to the house. She sat by the hearth, her brown hair pulled back in a braid with damp tendrils sticking to her neck and her mouth pressed in a thin line of frustration as she worked.

She'd grown taller over the last few months, and thinner. Her wrists looked like sticks and her shoulders were lumpy, like sharp roots were sprouting from her skin. It was just bone, though. We were all made of bone these days.

16

"Good morning," I said, wondering what had caused the scowl on her face.

"I'm up," she said. "You don't have to make nasty comments."

"It wasn't a nasty comment," Jonn said, bumping her foot with his good leg.

Ivy frowned. She'd become more surly lately, which could have been due to growing taller while eating less.

I checked the stew over the fire. It would cook all day and be ready to eat for supper. In the meantime, we could have potatoes for breakfast. I put them at the edge of the coals to bake.

After a few moments of work, my sister growled in frustration. "This stupid yarn," she said, tossing it down. "I'm so *sick* of it."

"Are you sick of eating, too? Because that's what we have to give up if we can't make quota," I snapped.

Tears prickled her eyes. "You're so mean. Why can't you be like Ma?"

The words hurt like slaps. "I'm sorry I haven't been more cheerful while I'm trying to keep you alive," I said finally.

Her eyes glimmered with unshed tears. She crossed her arms. I wondered for the thousandth time what was wrong with her these days.

"While we weave, I'll tell you riddles," Jonn said. "All right?"

She rubbed her arm across her eyes and lifted one shoulder in a shrug. She didn't look at me. "All right."

I stalked to the kitchen and braced myself against the stove. I bit my lip to keep from saying the words that filled my mouth.

I wanted to slap her. Fulfilling quota wasn't a choice. It wasn't something we did because we wanted to, or because we enjoyed it. This was do or die. If we

17

didn't deliver our required amount of yarn to the village each week, we didn't receive our food supplies—supplies that were already being rationed because of the Farther occupation. If we didn't make quota, we wouldn't be fed.

My sister was almost fourteen years old—almost a grown woman in our world. She knew this. She had to know it. We had no other choice.

"I'm going into the village," I announced, and headed for the door.

TWO

THE FROST WAS cold. Ice wrapped the tree branches in soft silver, and a mist of shadow and snow enveloped the woods like a veil. The path was long and twisting, and I ran.

My cloak streamed behind me, a ribbon of blue in a world of white. All around me, the snow fell in slow spirals like fairy dust. It might be beautiful in some other place. Here it was ominous, because here we had no fairy tale endings...only horror stories.

Blue blossoms lined the path, the flowers that kept the monsters in the forest at bay. But as I headed for the village, Watchers weren't the first thing on my mind.

There were other things to be worried about in the Frost now.

Farthers.

My stomach twisted at the thought, and I slowed. I didn't want to go into the village, but I had no choice. That rabbit wouldn't feed us for two more days. We needed more food.

Silence blanketed the trees and clung to the snow the closer I got to the village. Not even bluewings stirred in the branches above my head. I knew what had the creatures so disturbed. Our home had been invaded. The balance, precarious as it had been, was completely upset. Two months ago, Gabe had stumbled through the Frost and into my life. But now he was gone.

I had stayed.

And so had the Farther soldiers who'd come looking for him.

My boots crunched in the snow as I stepped over a fallen limb and ducked under a low-hanging bough. The path curved around a cluster of trees, their branches reaching for me like skeletal hands. As I rounded the curve, I stopped.

Soldiers stood in the path, rifles slung across their arms. Their heads turned in unison as they caught sight of me, and I forced myself to keep walking. My hands were suddenly clammy with sweat despite the frigid wind, and my skin prickled.

Here the path became enclosed on all sides by a cage-like tunnel made of thick metal slats interwoven with wire. The Farther soldiers guarded the entrance, armed with guns. They were here to make sure no Watchers slipped down the path to the village, they said. They were here for our safety, they said.

As if anyone believed such a lie.

I swallowed to moisten my dry throat. My footsteps rang out too loud in my ears as I reached the entrance to the chute of ribbed metal that snaked through the forest like a skeletal dragon's trachea. The Cage, we'd started calling it, for that was what entering it made us feel like. Like animals, trapped.

Villagers dotted the path inside the Cage, mostly woodsmen and hunters coming or going from their daylight work in the forest or along the shores of the nearby river or lake of ice. Most kept their faces turned toward the ground and away from the soldiers' stares. Nobody spoke.

I stepped into the Cage. The metal bars above and around me blocked some of the light, but still let in the searing wind. I tugged my cloak tighter around me at the moment of scrutiny. I hated it. Every second I walked the tunnel of cold steel, I imagined the soldiers raising their weapons and shooting me in the back. What if they'd somehow discovered that I was the one who'd sheltered Gabe? What if they knew that I'd helped him escape? Would they wait for me to show up for Assembly or quota day and then nab me like a rabbit?

I forced myself to take a few deep breaths, to be calm.

Then a figure in a blue cloak caught my eye.

He stood only a few paces away, leaning against the metal supports of the Cage as he adjusted the snow blossom-emblazoned leather strap on his wrist. A young man. He turned his face as I drew close, and I knew him at once.

Adam Brewer.

He was tall and lean, dark-haired, with eyes that pierced like arrows and a mouth that rarely smiled. He always seemed to wear a look of intense concentration, as if he were solving all the Frost's puzzles behind those dark eyes of his.

My heart thudded. Adam and I shared a deadly secret, one we didn't dare speak of in public. Adam was a Thorns operative—a member of a secret organization dedicated to the overthrow of the corrupt and cruel Aeralian dictatorship that had killed and imprisoned many. If the Farthers knew who he was, they would shoot him without hesitation. Yet here he stood, fearless, while the Farther soldiers stamped their boots to ward off the cold only a few paces away.

Our gazes met.

A muscle twitched in his jaw, as if he had something he wanted to say but restrained himself. The air between us thickened, and I felt his attention as tangibly as if he'd put his hand on my arm. I itched to acknowledge him, to say his name, to ask if he had news, any news. He was my one link to Gabe, to the Thorns, to my parents' double life...to everything that had happened.

But I couldn't. I couldn't speak to him here or in the village, where people still supposed us to be enemies. And I hadn't seen him alone in the forest since the night Gabe disappeared through the portal.

I ached with the weight of a million questions. I wanted to ask him about Gabe, about the gate, about my parents. About what he was doing now, about what he planned to do in the future. I'd become someone else, someone adrift in a sea of secrets and conspiracies, and he was an island of answers and knowledge and strength.

But the back of my neck prickled with awareness of the Farthers behind us. My mouth felt locked shut.

Adam's eyes slid over me as I passed.

My hopes of speaking with him, asking him any questions at all, hardened and shattered as I continued down the path through the Cage. The wind bit at my gloved fingers and tugged the edges of my cloak, and I walked faster, my feet making wet crunching sounds in the snow.

I turned another corner made of ribbed steel, and I stole a glance behind me.

He was gone.

I blinked once and looked ahead. Now I could see the stone roofs of the village peeking above the trees. I was almost to Iceliss. Fresh dread broke over me, and anxiety began to gnaw at my stomach as I reached the village gate.

Metal spikes stabbed the sky where our wooden walls had once stood, and the village entrance had been transformed into a web of steel cages that locked at sundown, keeping dangerous things out...and other dangerous things in. Soldiers patrolled the top of the gate from a walkway that led around the entire perimeter of the village. Their eyes were hidden by the black eyeshades they wore, but I still felt the weight of their gazes on me, and I shuddered at the sight of the guns in their hands.

The shadows cast by the Farther walls slid over my skin as I slipped through the gate. I passed beneath the soldiers, and then I was inside the village.

The stone streets and houses looked different now. Older, sadder. Farther soldiers were everywhere. The snow in the streets was churned into muddy sludge by their boots. The quota yard was full of them lounging, talking, and smoking.

Clutching my cloak around me, I headed for the market. I didn't like to linger here.

"Lia!"

My best friend, Ann, darted from a shop and slipped her arm into mine. Her bright red cloak made a brave splash against the gray stone of the buildings around her, but her cheeks gleamed pale and dark circles ringed her eyes. In the last two months, she'd gone from rosy to gaunt. Her father, the Mayor, was collaborating secretly with the Farthers. He'd sold his own people out to the enemy, and she bore the horrible knowledge in secret. For all the rest of the village knew, he was as much a victim as the rest of us.

I hugged her tightly. "I didn't know if I'd see you today."

Our friendship was like that now, meted out in snatches of conversation and furtive whispers. It wasn't safe. Nothing was safe anymore.

"I snuck out," she said, glancing past me at the soldiers in the quota yard. "Father is busy kissing Raine's boots, as usual." Her gaze flicked over me, and her eyebrows knitted together as she frowned. "What are you doing here? There isn't an Assembly I don't know about, is there?"

"We need cornmeal. Ivy's going through a growth spurt." The fact that everyone's allotted food rations had been decreased wasn't helping, either, but since Ann's father had given that order, I didn't bring it up to her.

Ann squeezed my hands in hers, and her gaze dropped to the ground. She knew. I could see the shame in the way she hunched her shoulders, as if against a chill in the wind.

"Walk with me?" she murmured, flicking another glance at the soldiers.

We crossed through the center of the village, where the shops and houses of stone crowded together as if huddled against the cold. Pale lichen covered the rooftops and walls, and painted snow blossoms adorned every house, carved into the doors and on the posts and thresholds. Horse-drawn carts rattled past over the cobblestoned streets, where the stones were arranged in patterns of blue blossoms surrounded by gray. A faint dusting of dirty snow coated everything.

"Did you hear the latest news?" she hissed, as soon as we were past the soldiers and out of earshot.

Apprehension knotted in my belly. I shook my head mutely.

"Watchers. They prowled the walls last night, testing them."

My apprehension turned to anger. "It's the Farthers and their guns, their technology," I said. "They're stirring everything here into a frenzy. The Watchers never came to the walls of the town before they arrived."

She hesitated. "Perhaps so, but Raine is only using this to further his own cause. He told the Circle of Elders just last night that this only proves his soldiers are necessary—to protect us from the Watchers. He says that with their guns and technology, they can keep us safer than we've ever been."

"And they believed him?" I couldn't believe it. "The Farthers are creating the problem and then offering themselves as the convenient solution. Surely the Circle sees this?"

Ann shook her head. "I don't know what they think anymore. The Elders have become more reticent. They're frightened for their livelihoods, their families. They do and say little at the gatherings besides sitting there like rabbits. My father does most of the talking, or Raine."

I shook my head in disgust.

She bit her lip and leaned closer. "There's more, although this bit hasn't been announced to the village yet. The Farthers are building a consulate in the center of the village. They've already discussed plans with my father, and laborers arrived this morning from across the river. They start work this week."

"A...a consulate?" My mind spun with confusion. "You mean...?"

She lowered her voice to a whisper. "I mean they plan to stay."

The words hit me like a punch in the stomach. For months now, we'd been promised a peaceful resolution to this waking nightmare. The Farthers had entered our land and occupied our village under the claims of searching for a fugitive, but as time passed it became increasingly obvious that they had more on their minds than finding one person. And now they were bringing in laborers?

I grabbed Ann's wrist. "Tell me exactly what this means."

"A consulate building can only mean that they're sending an official representative from Aeralis to govern us. My father will be a puppet ruler, and some Farther diplomat will be calling the shots."

Official, Aeralis, govern, puppet... My knees weakened, my hands felt numb. "And what dos the Circle say about *that*?"

"Like I said, the Elders don't say much these days. I've seen them leaving the house late at night, accompanied by soldiers to 'see them home safe,' Father says. It's a show of power. They know they don't dare speak out. They've been silenced."

Sharp talons of panic closed around me, squeezing the breath from my lungs. If the Circle—a governing body specifically formed for justice and protection—wouldn't fight against the Farthers and their unjust occupation of our village, who would?

We passed the Assembly Hall. I paused beside one of the relief carvings, painted blue like the sky-colored snow blossoms of the Frost. I darted a glance around. "And what about Watcher attacks? Aren't the Farthers afraid?"

She leaned against the wall and brushed a gloved hand over her eyes. "I heard Officer Raine telling my father that they plan to continue reinforcing the gates and walls. They're going to bring more guns to protect themselves."

"Fools," I muttered. More guns meant more Watchers buzzing around the forest, agitated and

26

aggressive. "They're going to stir the monsters into a frenzy if they start poking around with their technology, and then who will pay? Us." I thought of my family's farm, lonely and isolated against a backdrop of frozen trees. Who would defend us if the Watchers tried to break down our door?

Ann played with the strings on her bonnet. "Listen. There's one more thing I heard."

I straightened and cast another glance around to make sure no one could hear. "What?"

She traced the embroidery on the edge of her cloak with one finger. "The officer told my father that...that they have finally confirmed the identity of the Thorns operative working in the Frost."

All the air left my lungs. I felt as if I'd been punched. *Did they know about Adam? Did they know about ME?* My eyes flew to hers, but she stared at a patch of ice on the ground and didn't look up.

"They said it was Cole Carver."

My legs trembled in relief. Not Adam. Not me. The words began to sink it, though, and my lip curled. "Cole? But everyone knows the Watchers killed him."

And as far as anybody else knew, the truth was as simple and tragic as a careless boy in a dangerous forest. The whole village had mourned. I remembered his parents, their faces blotchy with grief as they absorbed the news Adam Brewer had gently delivered to them. I remembered the townsfolk gathered in a hushed circle around them, sorrowful over a life extinguished so young, and the funeral two days later where everyone spoke glowingly about his bravery and kindness. I'd even said a few words about my former friend, the sly and flirtatious boy who hadn't been able to resist hunting in the Frost during the night despite its dangers, and everyone had nodded and wiped away tears and whispered to each other that he'd intended to marry me, and wasn't it terribly sad?

In fact, the villagers had been giving me sympathetic looks for the last two months, thinking I grieved his death and my inevitable spinsterhood. Nobody but Adam, his family, and mine—and Ann—knew the grim truth. Cole had betrayed us. He'd followed us into the Frost, intending to expose Adam and me to the Farthers for helping Gabe escape. He'd held us at gunpoint and threatened to shoot me. But he'd been snatched up by a Watcher before he could deliver on his threat, and eaten.

I remembered the sickening crunch of bone when the monster struck from the shadows, the spray of blood on the snow, the screams. I pressed a hand over my eyes, willing the memories away.

"They never recovered his body," Ann reminded me. "And that isn't so unusual, but one of the Farther officers told my father that he believes Cole escaped along with the fugitive. He said he thinks the rest of us are too stupid to have been involved."

She sounded angry, but I felt light as air. If the Farthers thought the only Thorns agent was gone, that meant they wouldn't suspect Adam. They wouldn't suspect *me*.

My family would be safe.

The knot of apprehension in my chest eased a little.

"Good," I told her. "If they think we're clever, they'll be that much more on their guard. It's good they aren't expecting us to be smart."

"Well, it infuriates me," she whispered. "It makes my blood boil when I think that traitorous Cole Carver gets the credit for all your bravery and good deeds, even if it's only in the eyes of the Farthers."

I looked at my boots. She didn't know about Adam and his true involvement with the Thorns. In fact, for all she knew, he and I still distrusted and hated each other. Two months ago I'd believed Adam's family responsible for my parents' deaths, until I found out that Cole had killed them and blamed the Brewers. Ann knew now that Cole had killed my parents, and that I had helped Gabe escape with the assistance of the Thorns, but I'd kept the rest of the operatives'—Adam and his family's—identities a secret.

Secrets kept us safe.

The weight of the knowledge I kept from her pressed heavily on me, though, and I ached to tell her everything—Adam, my parents, the extent of the secrets that permeated our village.

But I couldn't.

"Don't let it bother you," I said. "This is a good thing. If they suspect it was him, they won't be sniffing around for anyone else. This protects me."

"I know. It just rankles me all the same. And I suspect Officer Raine just wants the problem done with so he can report it taken care of. I think since Cole is dead and the fugitive is gone and there's been no sign of the Thorns for months now, they think everything is over." She paused. "And it is over, isn't it?"

I thought of the brooch hidden in the drawer of my bureau. Adam had issued me an invitation the night we'd taken Gabe to the gate, and I hadn't made a decision yet. The knowledge of that brooch burned in the back of my mind, making me restless and uneasy.

Realizing she was waiting for some kind of reply, I said, "It's over. He's gone, and he's not coming back."

She looked relieved, but I felt unbelievably empty saying the words out loud.

Gabe was gone, but everything had changed anyway. He'd been the catalyst, and now my entire world had turned upside down.

We reached the open-air market, where booths and stalls braved the snow and wind as their banners fluttered in the breeze, advertising their wares. I passed the stall where old woman Tamma sold herbs and medicines, and our gazes slid away from each other. I'd once bought medicine from her for Gabe, and ever since then I'd felt her watching me as if she knew something.

I tugged my cloak closer around my shoulders and headed for the food stalls. Here, families could trade their excess perishables in exchange for other goods, but during the cold winter months the offerings were meager and limited mostly to meat and fish. We had the cow and the chickens, and our stores of dried onions, turnips, potatoes, and apples from the short and brutish summer, but I didn't hunt and the traps yielded scant offerings. With my parents dead and the Farthers eating much of the extras, the food supplies we received in exchange for our quota were not enough these days.

I traded a knitted scarf and a pair of mittens for six small fish caught through a hole in the ice over the river. A steep price, but we needed the food. The seller wrapped them up, and I took the smelly bundle under one arm. He gave me a grim nod of solidarity, but when his eyes cut to Ann he scowled and muttered something under his breath.

Ann looked neither surprised nor offended. Just resigned.

I could feel the stares we were attracting. Or rather, the stares Ann was attracting. People murmured and frowned our way. A chill tickled the back of my neck, and I bit my lip. I hastily traded with another seller for a cup's worth of cornmeal and then grabbed Ann's arm to steer her back toward the village square.

"What was that about?" I demanded as soon as we'd left the market. "Why did he look at you that way?"

She played with the edge of her cloak. "My father's cooperation with the soldiers hasn't been popular with some, you might say."

I snorted. "A gross understatement. But you aren't your father."

Ann didn't reply to that. There was no need. We both knew how damning association with a traitor could be. "Did you hear about Everiss?" she asked instead.

"No, what's wrong?" Everiss was the eldest Dyer daughter, and more Ann's friend than mine, but I'd known her since our days in the village school.

"She's called off her betrothal."

I was shocked. The last time we'd spoken, Everiss had talked of nothing else but marriage and babies, and then she'd chided me repeatedly for not being betrothed myself.

"I don't know. She won't talk about it. The whole family is upset with her. It would have been a good match."

"Maybe she decided she loved someone else," I mused. And in my mind I saw Gabe's face, and my chest ached. But I pushed the thought away. He was gone.

I needed to move on with my life.

"Perhaps," Ann said, and looked over her shoulder as someone hissed something at her. "I should get back to the house, I think."

"It was good to see you," I said, glaring at the person who'd issued the muttered taunt at my friend. "Be safe."

She smiled ruefully. "I'm the one who should be saying that to you."

But I wasn't so sure anymore. These days, things seemed just as dangerous no matter which side of the village walls you lived on.

She slipped away, and I turned and headed for the gate to the Frost. The fish were heavy in my arms, but all I could think about was how they weren't heavy enough for the price I'd paid, and how tiny and frail Ann seemed now, as if a strong gust of wind would break her. When had her smile gotten so brittle? Was it after the Farther soldiers began to occupy the village, or even more recently?

Worry gnawed at my insides and muttered in my thoughts. I almost didn't hear the voice whispering my name.

"Pssst, Lia Weaver!"

I stopped.

The shadows in the alley to my left stirred. I turned toward the movement, uncertain. "Hello?"

"Quick. Over here."

I caught a glimpse of a flutter of black fabric and a flash of a hand beckoning.

I hesitated. The hand shot out and closed over my wrist, yanking me forward. Suddenly I was pressed against the side of a stone house with a cloaked figure clamping a hand over my mouth. Panic stabbed me. I kicked, biting at his hand.

"Calm down, girl."

"Then let go of me!"

He let go and stepped back. I jerked away.

My frenzy had dislodged his hood, and I blinked in recognition.

The blacksmith's middle son.

He was about my age. We'd gone to school together. I knew him, but only vaguely. We had never spoken.

"Leon Blacksmith?"

32

He released me and adjusted the hood of his cloak. His sharp blue eyes blazed with intensity as they met mine. A shiver ran up my spine and danced across my skin.

"I'm sorry about the subterfuge, but we can't be seen," he said.

I feigned ignorance as I bent to retrieve the bundle of fish and sack of cornmeal I'd dropped. "Why not?"

Instead of answering, he put a finger to his lips and motioned for me to follow him. Then he turned and hurried down the alley.

Whatever he had in mind, I didn't want any part of it. I turned to slip away, but his voice cut through the air. "*Please.*"

Sighing, I joined him. He rounded a corner and came to a stop behind a stack of firewood. We were obscured from the view of anyone in the streets, and no windows opened on this side of the house. I could see the wall around the village from where we stood, but the soldiers were too far away to hear anything.

"What's this about?" I demanded as soon as he stopped.

"Did you find her?"

I whirled. A pair of boys emerged from behind the woodpile. I only vaguely recalled their names. Seth Baker? One of the Hunter boys? A girl was with them, and I didn't know her except from a hazy recollection.

"Yes," Leon replied. To me, he said, "This is Seth, Bern, and Onna." He pointed at the girl, and she flipped her hair out of her eyes and gave me a toothy smile.

"What's going on?" I scanned their faces for some shred of indication about what they wanted.

"Did you tell her?" Onna asked.

Leon shook his head. He looked at me.

"I've heard good things about you, Lia Weaver," he said. "You're strong, you're clever, and you aren't squeamish when difficult things need to be done. You travel through the Frost several times a week, and you live far from the safety of the village walls. Rumor has it you've even seen a few Watchers out there."

"So?" I said, too uneasy to be flattered. I shifted the bundle of fish and cornmeal in my arms and stamped my feet to ward off the cold. "You want me to tell you a few creepy bedtime stories or something?"

They chuckled, although I hadn't really been trying to make a joke. "You're funny, too," Leon said. "But no. We want you to join us."

"Join you?"

"We're going to get rid of the Farthers," Onna interjected.

"What?"

They gazed at me solemnly, and I realized they were serious.

"How?"

"Listen," Leon said. "The soldiers are oppressing our village. They're eating our food and stirring up the Watchers and they're pushing us around. We're a free people! We don't have to put up with this. But our Mayor is under Raine's thumb. If anything's going to be done, we just have to do it ourselves. We're calling ourselves the Blackcoats—" He gestured at them all, and I noticed the black scarves and clothing they wore. "—and we're going to save this village."

I stared at them. They were nothing more than a couple of ragged young people with fervent expressions and clenched fists. "And how exactly do you plan to rid the village of Farther soldiers again?"

"Targeted acts of resistance," Leon said. "Stealing food, damaging property, leaving ominous messages."

"Leaving ominous messages?" I couldn't contain my derision. Were they stupid? "You think that will work against armed soldiers?"

"You know what I mean. We'll make it so unbearable for them to stay that the costs will begin to outweigh the benefits. If we aren't worth occupying, then they'll leave."

"Or retaliate," I said.

"It's worth the risk." Leon folded his arms. "Well?"

I was silent, chewing over my words. Finally—"Why me?"

He chuckled mirthlessly. "Like I said. You've got a reputation for being tough. And you have inroads that the rest of us don't."

"Inroads?"

Onna smirked. "You'll be perfect for when we target the Mayor. You know his daughter. We can sneak you in their house. Maybe you can even go after her, too. I'm thinking public humiliation—"

"Hold on." I took a step back and drew in a quick breath. "What does Ann have to do with any of this?"

"She's related to the traitor scum," she said. "So she's guilty by association."

"You must be joking." A flush crept up my cheeks, and heat pooled between my shoulder blades. "Ann doesn't agree with what her father does. And she has no control over who her parents are any more than you can help being a Blacksmith."

"Save the pathos for someone who cares," he sneered. "Ann Mayor has been hobnobbing with the Farther officers since they came here, along with her father. If you aren't willing to teach her a lesson, then you're out."

"All right," I snapped. "Then I'm out."

35

They all stared at me. Leon opened his mouth, but didn't say anything. Clearly they hadn't expected me to say that.

And clearly they didn't know me at all.

"Ann Mayor is my best friend." I stabbed a finger at Leon. "She has nothing to do with the Farther occupation, and she has no control over her father's actions, and I will not hold her responsible for the injustice that happens. And if any of you mess with her, you mess with me. Got it?"

Leon's eyebrows drew together in an angry slash above his nose. "I think you know the way back to the road."

"I think I do." I pushed past Onna.

"Wait," Leon said sharply.

I paused.

"If you walk away from this now, then you've made an enemy."

"Then consider me your nemesis," I growled.

I stared at him until he looked away. I was too angry to speak, so I didn't. I left him standing at the entrance to the alley as I headed for the Frost, and I didn't look back.

THREE

MY BLOOD WAS still simmering from the sting of Leon's comments when I got home, so I shoved the fish and cornmeal at Ivy without a word and went to the barn to check the animals. I brushed the horses' coats with short, hard strokes as their accusations ran through my head. Ann had no control over her father's choices, and she wasn't responsible for what had happened to the village. If people thought I was going to blame her for the Farther occupation, they were dead wrong.

I finished with the horses and threw the brush into the tack bucket so hard a puff of dust plumed up where it hit. With a growl of frustration, I wheeled to check on the cow.

And ran straight into Adam Brewer's arms.

"Brewer?" I jerked away and leaned against the stall door, rubbing my suddenly shaking arms. I hadn't heard him enter. Was he unnaturally quiet, or had my anger so absorbed my attention that I'd grown careless? "You startled me."

His eyes flicked to mine. He was calm, composed, and unreadable as always, but I sensed a hum of tension in him, a disquiet that made my skin prickle in answer. When he looked at me, I felt like he saw more than I wanted him to see. It unnerved me.

"I called your name," he said, his voice a rich whisper uncurling in the near-darkness.

I brushed away a lock of hair that had fallen into my eyes. It was something to do because I was suddenly too restless, too aware of the air surrounding me. Why did he have that effect on me?

"What are you doing here?"

"When I saw you today, it seemed like you wanted to speak to me. And I've been meaning to talk to you."

"Talk to me about what?"

But I had a feeling I already knew.

"When your parents were killed, they left a hole in the net of Thorns operatives."

My fingers found the wall, and I leaned against it. My legs had begun to tremble.

"You kept the brooch," he said, "but you gave me no definitive answer about your intentions."

I thought about the secret room beneath our feet filled with maps and documents. I thought about the location of the farm, far from the village and surrounded by forest. Of course they wanted me to work for them. It was perfect.

But what about my family?

"The safety of my siblings is my top priority," I managed.

Adam's eyes softened. "The work we do is dangerous. I won't pretend it isn't. But you might find that refusing to fight back against the Aeralian occupation is even more dangerous in the end."

"Is the Farthers' occupation of the Frost the Thorns' top priority?"

"No. But the defeat of the Aeralian dictator is, and if he is unseated, then your occupation will end, too." He paused. "But you forget—this is my home, too. And I will defend it with my life."

He was not native to the Frost, but he still seemed a part of it all the same. He'd lived here for years.

I considered his words. On the one hand, it was dangerous work with an uncertain end. But on the other, it was my parents' work, and it was noble. I believed that.

Adam was waiting for my reply.

"I don't know," I said, although the words themselves felt like a surrender to destiny. I lifted my eyes to his and I held his gaze even though doing so made my stomach drop to my knees. "But I will make a decision soon."

He accepted this answer. "If you need to communicate with me, hang a lantern by the tree line. That's the signal."

I remembered. We'd done the same the night Gabe had traveled through the portal. "I'll remember."

He nodded. He was still looking at me.

One of the horses snorted, and I turned to soothe him. When I turned back, Adam had vanished. The barn door was slightly ajar, and a cold wind fanned my cheeks.

I sighed.

~

Adam Brewer and his Thorns, Leon Blacksmith and his Blackcoats, the Farther soldiers and their consulate plans—the stress of it all pounded a headache behind my eyes as I settled down to work on quota with my siblings, but I did my best to act calm. Jonn seemed to sense my frustration, for he silently patted my arm a few times, a gesture that only made me seethe. Why did he always seem to think I was a glass bowl waiting to be broken these days?

Scowling, I filled the kettle with fresh snow from the yard and returned into the main room to hang it over the fire. Ivy's shoulders tensed as I drew close to her. We were still in a disagreement over quota.

Jonn studied both our faces before settling on mine, and I could read the warnings in his eyes. He jerked his chin at Ivy, urging me to speak, and I suppressed a sigh. Irritatingly sensitive or not, my twin always knew how to coax me into softening.

"I'm sorry," I said, trying to sound gentle. "You're right. I haven't been in a very good mood lately."

"Nobody is," Jonn added, ever the peacemaker. "The Farthers are making everyone tense."

My sister's eyes shimmered. She grabbed her yarn and bent over it. "Tell me some riddles?"

He glanced at me, silently urging me to participate.

I searched my mind for a riddle. "Uh...what brings danger and strife, but also relief and life? We are...uh...we are prisoners of it, yet protected by it."

"Snow," she answered immediately, with a sniff of triumph. She knew that one. It was one our father had told us often while we'd worked the quota as children.

"What tells stories with its fingers and keeps hunger at bay with its hands?" Jonn asked.

"A Weaver," Ivy said. "Because we spin yarns and fulfill our quota. Something harder, Jonn."

He pursed his lips, thinking. Then he smiled. "What, when kept sharp, may win you a wife, but when dull, may cost you your life?"

Her forehead wrinkled. "A kitchen knife?"

"How would a kitchen knife find you a wife?" I demanded.

She scowled. "I don't know. What's the answer, smart one?"

"Wit."

She stuck out her tongue at me, but the mood in the room was easing from icy to warmth. "You only know it

40

because Da always told you all the answers to all the riddles."

I rolled my eyes. "Hardly true."

"Well, here's one she doesn't know the answer to," Jonn said. "What woven secret will keep you warm?"

She pondered the question. "I don't know." She glared at me as if it were my fault. "What is it?"

I threw up my hands in exasperation. "I don't know, either—which just goes to show that he didn't tell me everything. Da always teased us with that one, remember?"

"Ma used to say it was love," he said.

"Well, I think it's yarn," I muttered.

"Yarn isn't a very romantic answer," she said.

"The riddle isn't 'what *romantic* secret will keep you warm.'"

"Still—"

"I don't think there is a single answer," Jonn interrupted. "Da loved to tease, and he liked to see us try to puzzle things out. Especially smarty over there." He nodded at me. "Drove her nuts not knowing the answer to every riddle."

I snorted to show my derision at such a claim.

She smiled hesitantly, and the mood in the room warmed.

The kettle began to squeal, and I got up to make tea. "Keep working," I said when Ivy showed signs of slowing.

She stuck out her tongue, and as quickly as that the mood was ruined again.

Jonn shook his head at me, and I bit back a sigh of frustration.

My mind returned to my conversation with Adam in the barn, and apprehension gnawed at my stomach.

41

He wanted an answer, but I didn't know what to tell him.

I was working myself to the bone just trying to make ends meet and keep my family from starvation. How could I do anything else, dire as things were?

~

That night, I crept out of bed and dug in my drawer for the Thorns brooch that had belonged to my parents. The silver branch glittered like ice in the near darkness as I turned it over, and in my mind's eye I saw Adam's face as he handed it to me two months ago. "You'll need it," he'd said.

And yet, so far I'd done nothing.

I closed my palm around the piece, feeling the sharp sensation of the cold metal against my hand, thinking hard of my ma and da's faces. Pain filled my chest and burned at the back of my eyes. With a hiss of frustration, I shoved it back in the drawer beneath my socks, threw back the quilt, and padded to the window that overlooked the yard below.

The moon cast a silver glow over everything, and through the frost on the glass, the forest made a black smudge against the stark white of the snow. I pressed my forehead against the chilled glass and breathed out slowly.

I didn't know what to do.

The shadows shifted and rippled, and I caught the faintest glimmer of red light glancing off the snow. A Watcher? Or simply my imagination coupled with my exhausted mind?

I stared at the spot where I'd seen movement until my eyes ached as I strained for the sound of claws against the snow, but the night was silent.

My sister's breathing filled the room in a steady rasp, and my mind spun a memory of Gabe bundled in quilts by the fire, his hair damp against his feverish forehead and his mouth moving as he mumbled deliriously. My throat squeezed at the thought of him, and I shifted restlessly on the window seat.

When shivers overtook me from the cold and my own loneliness, I returned to my bed and huddled under the quilts until dawn.

~

By the next mandatory Assembly, my thoughts were still in turmoil. Dark clouds clotted the horizon and plunged the Frost into a state of near-twilight as I ran on the paths, my every sense attuned to the sounds of the forest. Nothing except a few bluewings stirred in the trees, and I reached the Cage out of breath but unscathed as always.

Ann waited for me by the gate. A thin line of red traced her cheek, the mark accentuated by her pale skin.

I frowned at the mark. "What happened to your face?"

"Oh, it's nothing," she stammered, brushing her fingers over the place. But it smudged red. I grabbed her shoulders and turned her toward the sun so I could see better.

"You're *bleeding*."

"It's nothing." She pulled free and smoothed her dress. Her expression was carefully guarded. "Just a little rock, that's all."

A ROCK? My pulse hammered, and my fingers curled into fists. I took a deep breath to steady myself. "Did one of the soldiers—?"

"It wasn't a Farther," she interrupted.

I snapped my gaze to the street. I saw a few sullen-looking children skulking around one of the shops, but none of them held stones. They wouldn't meet my eyes.

"Who, then?"

She shook her head. "Let's just go. Please. We'll be late."

I let it drop because she was right, we were going to be late, but I wasn't done with the topic. I hooked my arm in hers and together we hurried for the Assembly Hall.

Villagers streamed through the carved blue doors to the hall, their faces haggard and their bodies bundled in cloaks the colors of snow and frost. We slipped through the crowd without speaking and into the building. The air had already grown hot inside, and the room buzzed with low, urgent voices. Everything smelled faintly of sweat and damp wool. We took seats at the back.

A knot of soldiers strode past, and the presence of one man in particular made everyone shiver and turn their faces away as he limped past.

Officer Raine, the Farther officer in charge of the occupation.

His iron-gray cloak swept the floor behind him, and the decorations on the chest of his uniform glittered in the pale sunlight as he strode through the crowd. His uniform strained across the front of his chest, and the gloves on his hands were dirty. His left leg was weak from an old injury, and he lurched with every step he took.

Outwardly he looked benign, almost sad.

But the glint in his eyes made shudders run over my skin like a thousand tiny spiders.

Officer Raine's gaze raked over the villagers as if looking for signs of dissent. He reminded me of a cat

44

hungrily eyeing a nest of mice. His lip curled, and he snapped his fingers for the soldiers to flank him.

I stared at the floor until he'd moved on.

After Raine had taken his place beside the dais, the Mayor entered. Farther soldiers followed at his back, hanging back a little to make it look as though they were guarding instead of escorting him. But I knew the truth. He was their prisoner, and he dared not defy them. His skin looked almost gray, and deep shadows ringed his eyes.

Beside me, Ann inhaled sharply and squeezed my hand at his appearance. "He seems unwell," she whispered.

One of the soldiers turned his head and looked at us, his eyes finding her face in that brief heartbeat of a moment, and she shrank against me. I sat up straighter and put my arm around her. I didn't flinch as I met his gaze.

He moved on. I pressed my lips together in an effort to keep my expression neutral as I turned my face to the front of the room.

The Mayor stepped onto the platform and motioned for silence. The murmur of voices swelled and then quieted, and a tense silence swept the room.

"My people," he said quietly. "We have a grave matter to discuss."

Was I the only one who noticed how his hands trembled? I sat up straighter, frowning. He always began Assembly by reading the marks, our silly form of shaming those who didn't keep all the little rules. Why was he changing it?

A glance at Ann confirmed that her father's behavior had her mystified, too.

I opened my mouth to ask her when the door to the hall flew open, and more Farther soldiers entered. They dragged a man between them. I saw a patch of brown hair, a white face. Blood dripped from his nose.

Everyone gasped, and Ann grabbed my arm. "That's Edmond Dyer, Everiss's father."

The whole room watched, spellbound, as the soldiers hustled the man to the platform and dumped him down at the Mayor's feet. He lay in a heap, his head in his hands, groaning.

"Edmond Dyer," the Mayor said, looking down at the man. He spoke in a monotone, as if he were reciting a list of rules. "A friend to many in this town, a loyal member of this community...or so we thought."

Edmond lifted his head. "Please..." he rasped.

One of the Farther soldiers kicked him, and he crumpled again. Rage began to simmer in my stomach. Ann's grip on my arm tightened. The people around me muttered in outrage, but no one moved.

"Edmond has trespassed against the safety of this town," the Mayor said.

Trespassed against the safety of the town? What did that mean? What was his crime?

"As punishment, his property has been confiscated. He will serve a sentence of hard labor. His family will not be implicated in his crimes."

Gasps echoed all over the room as the words sunk in. His property, confiscated? Sentenced to hard labor? What could he possibly have done to merit this?

Property was only taken from a member of the village if they were proven to be physically or mentally unfit to maintain it, or if they directly defied the orders of the Elders. What had Edmond Dyer done?

I craned my neck, looking for Everiss, but I couldn't spot her curly brown hair anywhere. Instead I saw Dan Tailor, her former suitor. He sat hunched over in his

46

chair, one hand clenched in a fist with the knuckles pressed against his mouth like he was holding in a shout.

"Our...*coexistence*...with the Farthers has not always been easy, but it is necessary that we remain calm and continue to cooperate," the Mayor said. "We must not tolerate attempts to sabotage this cooperation."

"What cooperation?" I muttered, looking hard at the Farther soldiers flanking him.

Ann pressed her fingers into my arm, reminding me to remain silent.

"Take him away," the Mayor ordered hoarsely. His expression was blank, but he shut his eyes when the soldiers stepped past to hoist Edmond Dyer up again. He sagged between them like his legs were made of straw.

"Please," Edmond begged, this time addressing the crowd. His voice was raspy and low, tortured. "Please...I didn't..."

Every single villager sat frozen, stunned.

Why was no one standing up? Why was no one demanding an explanation, a trial? I felt myself rising from the bench, but Ann yanked me back down.

"Don't be stupid," she hissed in my ear, fierce and un-Annlike. "He'd throw you to the Farthers without blinking, just like he's doing to Edmond Dyer. Think of Jonn and Ivy."

The Farther soldiers grabbed Edmond's arms and yanked him toward the door. He shrieked once, a shrill sound of complete agony. The heavy oak door slammed, and the sound reverberated through the room.

I gripped the edge of the bench so tightly that my knuckles turned white, and I bit down on my lip hard enough to taste blood. Wasn't this what we'd always feared might happen?

It was the stuff of nightmares.

Beside me, Ann shivered. Her eyes were squeezed shut.

At the front of the hall, the Mayor grimaced and cleared his throat. "Let us continue," he said, adjusting the collar of his shirt and darting a glance at Officer Raine. "There are other matters on the agenda today."

No one moved. The whole room seemed mesmerized as we waited for him to continue.

"Our Aeralian friends have been with us for several months now, as you know, and I have just received word that an official representative will be joining us here."

The consulate Ann had spoken about?

Murmurs swept the room, and the Mayor held up a hand to call for quiet. The sounds died away, and he bared his teeth in another smile. But his control was slipping, and I could read the fear in his eyes. Whether that fear was of us or the Farthers, I couldn't tell.

"This representative will be here to ensure our safety. This is for the good of our town, and for the good of the Frost."

The villagers around me shifted and whispered, and an undercurrent of ugly anger filled the air. But no one said anything.

"Don't," Ann whispered to me sharply as I inched forward on the bench.

"Laborers will construct a place for the Aeralian representative," the Mayor continued. "They are dangerous, and not to be spoken with. They'll live and sleep in their own camps, and you are not to engage with them."

The silence was deafening. My blood had begun a slow, anxious boil in my veins.

He paused. "Now, let's read the marks, shall we?"

~

I almost ran from the building when we were dismissed. Fire burned beneath my skin and in my cheeks. I kept my mouth clamped shut, and I ducked my head down as I passed the Farthers standing guard at the door so they couldn't see the expression in my eyes.

Outside, the icy air fanned my cheeks. Pulling Ann behind me, I skirted the crowd and stepped into an alley between two shops.

"We have to do something." The memory of Edmond Dyer's shriek was burned in my mind forever. I began to pace. "Why was he arrested? Did you overhear anything from your father?"

"I don't know. I haven't heard even a whisper about this before now. And it doesn't make any sense." She wiped her thumb along the edge of her eye, brushing away a gathering tear. "The Elders' Circle is supposed to convene for any discipline against a villager, and they haven't. They usually come to see my father, or he meets them at the Assembly Hall. There has been no deliberation, I'm sure of it."

"Officer Raine ordered it, didn't he?"

She said nothing, but I could see by her expression that she thought I was right.

My stomach churned. I could barely see straight. "There was no warning, no trial, not even any specification about his crimes... And what about the rest of the family? What will happen to them? Their home was confiscated!"

She shook her head. "They'll be spread around to other families, I suppose. I should find Everiss."

"We have to do something," I snapped.

"What can we do?"

Resolve burned in the pit of my stomach.

I could do something.

49

"Yes," I said, grabbing her hands and squeezing them to make her focus. "Find Everiss and make sure she's all right. Let me know if there's anything I can do for them later. But right now, I need to go."

If I didn't get out of town now, I'd do something I'd regret. I could feel it in my bones.

"Lia," Ann began.

I met her eyes, and her face crumpled. She wrapped me in a quick, fierce hug.

"I couldn't bear it if anything happened to you," she whispered against my shoulder. "So be careful."

I gave her a squeeze in answer and then stepped back. "I'll see you soon."

She stood motionless, watching me as I hurried away.

FOUR

I FELT AS though I was engulfed in a dark cloud and I couldn't see a way out of it. I needed to get away and clear my head before I did something rash, something stupid. My boots kicked up a spray of snow as I rushed through the Cage for the Frost, and home. The wind blew in my eyes, stinging them and making them water. Or was it tears?

The trees closed over my head, obscuring the sky, and I was just a scrape of blue in a sea of white as I took the path home. Trampled snow blossoms littered my way, looking like bits of fallen sky embedded in the snow. I brushed my fingers over the blossoms dangling from my neck, my nervous habit, and hurried faster.

The farm came into view as I crested the final hill, and I stopped to catch my breath. A tendril of smoke curled from the chimney of the white clapboard house that stood alone in the center of the yard, surrounded by a skirt of snow. Footprints perforated a trail from the front door to the barn and back. Ivy must have seen to the animals already.

I needed a moment before I went into the house. I turned and plunged off the path into the Frost.

The icy branches enfolded me in an evergreen embrace. Snow swirled in my eyes and dusted my hair as I pushed through the icy vegetation in the direction of the traps. I walked quietly, keeping my ears tuned for any unusual sounds. The wild, white beauty of the forest made my chest ache. My breath burned in my lungs—it always felt colder in the Frost itself.

The traps were all empty. I swallowed curse words and turned for home. And all the dark, broken thoughts and fears swept over me like a muddy wave. Every single piece of my life had crumbled. My parents were dead. Gabe was gone. Farthers had occupied our village. And now my best friend might be in trouble, too.

I felt so helpless.

I stepped on a branch, and the rotted wood snapped like a shot beneath my boot. I paused and scanned the trees around me out of habit, and the feeling of being watched that always hovered at the edge of my awareness in the Frost slipped across my skin. I exhaled. My heart beat faster. And I realized I was looking—hoping—to see a flutter of blue cloak, a head of dark hair.

But he wasn't there.

My whole body went still as an idea came to me, clear as a rush of cold wind.

I let my lips curve into a grim, determined smile.

~

Jonn watched me all through dinner, his eyes narrowed. He read my moods better than anyone, and I was sure he'd sensed my sour temper. I swallowed the dry bits of potato and kept my gaze on my plate. Across the table, Ivy toyed with her food and jiggled her foot beneath the table.

We were a silent bunch.

"How are things in town?" Jonn asked when I thought I was about to scream from the weight of the unspoken words and my anxieties pressing against me.

I shot a glance at my sister. "Assembly was, well... Ivy, can you put more water over the fire for the tea?"

"You can say it in front of me," she snapped. "I'm not a child anymore. What happened at Assembly?"

I bit my lip and looked at my twin. He fumbled with his fork a moment before nodding, and I dragged in a deep breath. "They arrested Edmond Dyer. They took away his home and his livelihood and sentenced him to hard labor."

"What?" Jonn's knife clattered against the table. "Why?"

"The Mayor fed us a ridiculous story about him endangering the village." Just repeating it made my throat prickle and my skin itch with fury. "Farther soldiers threw him to the ground, kicked him, dragged him away... I'm glad you weren't there to see it, either of you."

They both blinked at me, stunned.

"And what do you think they really arrested him for?" Jonn demanded.

"A show of power...retaliation... They're trying to frighten us all into submission." Anger surged through me, making my hands shake as I gathered up my utensils and piled them on my empty plate. I thought of what else had happened, Leon and the rest—I had much more to tell Jonn, but not in front of my sister.

Ivy pressed her fingers over her mouth. "Are they going to take our farm away, too?"

"What? No. Of course not." I grabbed my empty plate and stood. My stomach still twisted with hunger, but we'd eaten all I dared spare from our food supply for the day. We would just have to tighten our belts until we got the weekly rations. I gathered up an armful of dishes and carried them to the kitchen. I dropped them in the sink and leaned against the wall, closing my eyes.

I needed to leave the signal for Adam to see. I took the lantern down from the hook on the wall and reached for the matches.

"I need to get something in the barn," I said, heading for the door.

Ivy sat white-faced, shaking in her chair, and Jonn was trying to calm her down. They barely heard me.

I ducked outside. The wind had kicked up again, bringing a flurry of snowflakes with it, and the specks of white danced before my eyes and melted against my lips. Above my head, the Watcher Ward danced and clattered. The sun had shrunk to a glowing coal behind the snow clouds, and a bluish haze bathed everything in twilight.

Swallowing to ease the dryness that filled my mouth and throat, I lifted the lantern and headed for the trees. When I hung out this lantern, I would signal Adam. He would come. And I would give him my answer.

Was I really ready to do this?

My footsteps were wet snapping sounds in the thick silence, and the wind trailed cold fingers through my hair. I stopped by the trees and fumbled for a match, striking it twice before the flame sputtered to life. I hung the lantern on a branch, and the halo of light it cast illuminated a hard circle of white around me but did nothing to penetrate the wall of shadows that signaled the beginning of the Frost.

Prickles crawled over my skin as I stared once more into the mouth of the Frost, straining to hear and see what lurked beyond, testing my own resolve as I stood there, facing the brink of night and the promise of Watchers. Whispering sounds slid from the trees as the wind whipped through the branches and moaned over the snowdrifts. A mothkat screeched in the distance.

Somewhere far away amid the shadows, past the safety of the tree line, a branch snapped, and my nerves drew taut as a bowstring. I poised for flight, quivering like a startled doe, bathed in the lantern light and exposed.

Two figures emerged from the trees. My heartbeat tripled. I reached for my knife as I scanned their faces. A boy and a girl. Both thin, almost waifish. Dark circles ringed their eyes, and their wrists were as slender as sticks.

"Please," the girl said, and lifted her arm. I sucked in a sharp breath when I saw the red marks crisscrossing her wrists. Angry, freshly healed wounds covered every inch of bare skin.

Then my gaze slid down, and I saw what she was holding. A crude pair of sticks tied together with twine.

The sign of the Thorns.

FIVE

I STARED AT the sticks in her hand as my pulse pounded in my ears and my head felt too light. Was this a trick? A trap? A clever ruse invented by Raine's men to catch me?

But no. The sign of the Thorns was secret.

They must have been sent here, just as Gabe was.

I looked at their skeletal bodies and their paper-thin rags, and they looked back with the kind of defiance hardened through beatings and starvation. Something in me squeezed so tight I couldn't breathe. Were children political prisoners now in Aeralis, too?

"I can help you. You're going to be all right," I said, doing my best to use my gentlest voice.

The girl made a soft sound like a kitten's mew. It might have been a sob.

"This way," I said. I took a step back and looked over my shoulder to make sure they were coming.

After a moment's hesitation, they followed. The girl held tightly to the boy's hand.

Thoughts ran circles in my head. They were Aeralians; the features were obvious, as were the clothes. I recognized the slick, synthetic fabric and the strange cut of the shirts. Had they crossed into the Frost themselves? Who had sent them? The same operative that sent Gabe?

I needed Adam. He would know what to do.

I took them to the barn.

The hinges creaked as I shoved the door open, and the children crept inside and huddled by the chicken cages, shivering and waiting for me to speak. They were like birds—timid, skittish, their hands fluttering restlessly. The clothing hanging from their bodies was far too thin for the weather. They needed blankets, scarves.

"Stay here," I said. "I'll bring you food and warmer things to wear. And don't worry—you're safe now."

The girl blinked at me.

Safe. I thought of Officer Raine and the rest of the Farther soldiers less than a mile away in the town. Did my words about safety sound as hollow to her as they did to me? Could this child ever feel safe again after what she'd been through?

"I'll be right back," I promised, and then I shut the door and leaned against it while I caught my breath. In my mind's eye, I saw the cuts on her arms. A shudder ran through me, and I pushed off the door and hurried to the house.

When I returned with milk and a stack of clothing and blankets, they were waiting, sitting together with their backs to the wall and their hands clasped.

"I brought you warm things. You'll sleep here tonight."

They took the clothing and stripped out of their rags, revealing their bodies. Skin stretched over bone. Bruises made purple patterns across ribcages, chests. Cuts told a story of unimaginable cruelty. My hands formed fists, but I hid them behind my back so the children wouldn't see them and think I was angry at them.

The girl dressed the boy first. Jonn's shirt and pants swallowed him up, and he looked at the sleeves flopping over his hands and made a barking sound like he was trying to laugh but had forgotten how. When she'd finished with him, the girl pulled on one of Ivy's nightgowns and turned to me expectantly.

"You can sleep here," I said, going to the middle of the room and crouching down to press the button for the trap door. The stone panel slid aside, revealing steps into a dark room below. "You'll be hidden."

"Safe," the girl said.

I nodded.

They climbed down the stairs slowly after me. A faint glow lit the room—a few of the phosphorus fungi from the deep Frost had burrowed into the cracks of the walls, and a bluish light tinged the air. I made them a bed of blankets and poured the milk into bowls. They looked so malnourished that I was afraid to give them anything more substantial.

"I'll be back tomorrow," I said. "Don't worry. A man is coming to help you. He'll take you somewhere safe."

The girl's lips parted in a ghost of a smile.

~

The fire cast red-gold light across Jonn and Ivy's faces as we worked silently on the quota. Outside, the wind howled and hissed across the snow.

Worry gnawed a hole in my stomach. I hadn't told them about the children in the barn. I'd hidden their dirty clothes in my quota basket and set out the lantern at the edge of the yard, but I hadn't spoken a word of it yet. I didn't know what to say.

Putting down the yarn, I paced to the window and peeked through the shutter at the yard. No snow fell from the sky tonight. Cool black shadows swathed everything, and a sprinkling of stars dusted the sky. At the edge of the yard, the lantern I'd hung earlier glowed against the trees like a single, captured firefly in the night.

Would Adam see it?

"You're restless," Jonn observed from his place beside the fire.

I tapped my fingers against the shutter, avoiding the question in his tone. "Ann said that Everiss and Dan are no longer betrothed."

His hands stilled. He looked up.

Ivy sighed loudly. "Everything is going wrong," she grumbled. "The Farthers, the village, even love is falling apart."

"Did Ann say why?" Jonn asked, and I didn't miss the way his eyebrows pinched together.

"No," I said. Why did he care about a bit of village gossip? Did he think the news made me miss Gabe? Did he think I would go crazy in a fit of lonely passion and leave them while I forged off in the Frost? "I don't know what happened between them, but either way it's unfortunate timing after what happened to her father today. The marriage would have helped her family significantly."

He frowned.

I glanced back at the lantern, and my breath caught in my throat.

Was that movement in the shadows? Adam?

My breath fogged the glass as I leaned closer and craned my neck. The fire crackled loudly in the silence behind me as I squinted.

Outside, a black shape rushed past the light and vanished.

I grabbed the windowsill, straining to see. My heart pounded against my ribs like a fist against a door.

Watchers?

The light of the lantern winked as another shape passed between it and us. A flash of spikes and fur. The gleam of long, powerful limbs. A low, trembling growl filled the air.

I sucked in a breath as cold swept over me. I eased the shutters shut and took a step back. My pulse throbbed in my throat. My fingers turned numb.

"What is it?" Ivy hissed. The yarn in her lap fell to the floor and rolled under a chair.

"Watchers. They're in the yard." I backed away from the window slowly.

Jonn grabbed the arms of his chair. "Are you sure?"

"I saw them," I insisted. "They were past the woods."

We were three points of a triangle—Ivy, Jonn, and me, frozen and facing each other. My thoughts swirled as I looked around the room. My blood buzzed with terror. The Aeralian children in the barn would be fine. They were safe below ground. I didn't know if I could say the same for us, trapped in this rickety farmhouse. The walls suddenly seemed perilously thin, the door a shred of wood, the windows delicate as ice.

"We're going to be fine," Jonn said, his tone low and calm like he was soothing a frightened animal. "The windows are covered by the shutters, and we've got plenty of snow blossoms beneath every window and beside every door. They'll look around and then they'll go away just like they always do. Perhaps they've come out to look for food, but they won't pass the blossoms for it."

Maybe he was right. I gulped air and sank down at the hearth.

Silence descended. We remained still, breathing shallowly, listening for any telltale sounds of footsteps, of snow sifting, of guttural snarls.

Nothing.

I sighed. Jonn smiled at me. Ivy relaxed and leaned back in her chair. Perhaps they'd already moved on. Perhaps I'd just imagined it in my worry-plagued mind. Too much anxiety, too little rest.

I started to rise—

CRACK!

Something slammed against the side of the house.

Ivy covered her mouth with both hands. Jonn jerked himself upright, his eyes wide. I ran to the mantle and fumbled with my father's ancient pistol that hung there.

"Ivy," I hissed. "Help Jonn into the bedroom and push the dresser in front of the door."

"But—"

"Help. Jonn. Into. The. Bedroom."

"No," he growled.

"Get in the bedroom and get under the bed, Jonn."

Another shudder shook the house. Dust fell from the rafters. In the kitchen, the pots shivered.

"Lia," he snapped, and for the first time his voice was less than calm.

Instead, I shot a glance at my sister. She scrambled to do what I said. She grabbed his arm and slipped it over her shoulders, helping him stand. A single look passed between my twin and me—every shred of pride and love and shame and self-loathing and fear in him poured from his eyes. He wasn't able to defend us. I shook my head at the protest I saw in his eyes. I just wanted him safe. Both of them.

The door to our parents' bedroom clicked shut. I heard the scrape of the dresser across the floor. I turned to face the door, the only point of entry I was really worried about. The bones of this house were strong. It was built from sturdy oak beams. But the door...

It'd been in disrepair since my father's death. The wood was old, weak. One well-placed blow from an angry Watcher might snap the lock, and throw it wide open.

I could hear the scrape of claws in the snow, the hiss of breath just outside the window. In my mind's eye I saw them—hulking black creatures with bristling, spiny backs, long necks, and glowing, blood-red eyes that shone in the night. I'd only gotten a good look at the monsters once, the night we took Gabe to the gate far in the Frost.

The night I'd seen one kill Cole Carver with one bite.

Why were they here now? What did they want?

My skin prickled all over as something scraped against the side of the house and dragged around it like the screech of a thousand fingernails. It went along the side and toward the door. The point of entry. The weak spot.

The room was too hot, too dark, too flickering, and lit only by firelight. My dress squeezed me, my throat hurt from holding my breath. My eyes were straining, and my ears were full of the sound of my own heartbeat.

The Watcher Ward that hung outside the front door clattered.

Would the monsters see the painted snow blossom symbol on the door, or would they bust right through?

I lifted the gun and braced myself. A bullet wasn't going to do anything, but I'd die before I'd run and hide and let the monsters come after my siblings without a fight. Maybe if they got me they'd think I was the only one, and they'd go away without searching further.

The hinges on the door squealed as something pressed against it. My pulse pounded. My mind was screaming at me. All the air left my lungs in one giant, terrified exhale. Sweat slipped into my eyes, and my hands were shaking so hard I could barely hold the gun. *Pleasedon'tpleasedon'tpleasedon't* was the only thing in my head.

I stared at the door, held my breath, and tried my best not to whimper.

And then...

Silence.

My hands sagged with the weight of the pistol, but I stayed standing, waiting for what felt like eons while the fire crackled and the wind howled against the cracks in the wall. Nothing outside stirred. An eternity ebbed and flowed in the absolute quietude as I waited.

Had they gone?

Or was this a cruel trick?

"Lia?" Ivy's voice trickled through the bedroom door. "What's happening?"

But I couldn't answer her. My eyes were glued to the door, the knob.

It was turning.

I lifted the gun again and squinted down the barrel. My heart was in my mouth. My blood was on fire. My legs trembled.

"Lia?"

The voice that called my named was muffled, but I still recognized it.

Adam Brewer.

SIX

ADAM STRODE INTO the room as soon as I unlatched the door, a swirl of snowflakes following him. Outside, the flakes drifted down gently in the darkness. A quiet snowfall, not a storm.

Adam's cloak swept the floor as he turned to trap me with his gaze, and his eyes burned with quiet intensity. He took in the sight of me, the gun in my hand, the absence of my siblings. He went back to the door and looked out, and a blast of icy wind fanned my cheeks and brought me back to a semblance of sanity.

"You're shaking," he observed quietly. "Not to mention the fact you're holding a weapon. Were you not expecting me?"

"Watchers," I managed, my voice rusty with relief. Seeing him standing there whole and uneaten when he'd been outside just moments ago squeezed the last bit of air from my lungs. The memory of blood on the snow flashed through my head again, and I blinked to banish it. I shut the door and leaned against it. "Didn't you see them?"

"There were tracks around the house, but the yard was empty." He turned to face me again, one hand braced against the door and one hand reaching for me. "You put out the lantern and I saw the light." He paused. "Are you all right?"

"Yes. No." The gun was too heavy in my hand now. I went to the mantle and put it back. The movements, precise and ordinary, restored my sanity and helped my hands to stop shaking. "I'm fine. It's just...they were slamming against the door. I can't imagine what might have—" I stopped. The children's clothing. It was in my basket—in the house—

I ran to the hearth and thrust my hand into the tangle of rags. My fingers brushed metal. I withdrew a locket and popped it open, and the glint of gears met my eyes.

Farther technology. It drew the monsters like bees to nectar.

My heart withered, but I smashed the locket under my shoe anyway. Our safety was more important than sentiment. I closed my eyes in silent apology, though, as I bent to pick up the pieces and put them back in the basket.

"You're sure you're all right?" Adam stepped close to me, reaching out a hand. He hadn't seen the locket.

"It's just been a long night." His intense scrutiny threatened to overwhelm me. I pressed a hand over my eyes.

"Lia!" Ivy's voice echoed faintly from behind the door. "What's going on?"

Adam turned his head in the direction of her voice, and his brow furrowed. He looked back at me and caught my panicked expression. "Should I go?"

"No, wait. It's all right if they know you're here. I—I need to speak with you," I said. I reached for his sleeve, but stopped before my fingers brushed against it. I didn't quite dare to touch him.

He crossed his arms and faced me. His dark eyes pinned me in place as always, and my skin prickled as always with a sensation that was not quite fear.

"I've got two Farther children hidden in the barn."

His eyes narrowed with sudden understanding.

"Lia!" Ivy shrieked. The dresser legs scraped behind the closed door as if she planned to emerge.

"We need to move them as soon as possible," he said.

"No, wait." I put both hands against his chest to block him from stepping toward the door. "The Frost. It's dark. The Watchers..."

"I don't think they'll come back tonight. And I have methods for...avoiding them."

I shook my head, adamant. "You're not going out there with just a few nets of snow blossoms. I don't know anyone who'd take that kind of risk."

"You did, once."

The words shut me up. I made a small noise in my throat, not quite agreement and not quite denial. Something hovered unspoken in the air between us— the memory of him standing as he waited for Gabe and me in the snow that night two months ago. That was what was in my mind. I didn't know what was in his.

Adam hesitated. His fingers stilled against the edge of his cloak, and then he removed it and passed it to me as if resigning something. "The morning, then. They'll be safe tonight."

Relief flowed through me. I hung his cloak on the rack and pointed toward the bedroom door that still shielded Ivy and Jonn. "I should let them know it's all right now."

Ivy threw her arms around me and sobbed when I opened the door. Behind her, my brother slumped against the bed frame, his face pale and his eyes angry. I met his gaze over her head, and an ocean of wordless things passed between us. I broke eye contact first, when Adam stepped to the doorway.

"Adam Brewer," Ivy gasped, her expression a mixture of accusation and frank curiosity. "What are you doing here?"

Jonn lifted his eyebrows and met my eyes with a firm stare that said he knew very well what Adam was doing here. I looked down at my hands.

Adam smiled faintly, assuming the diffident-Brewer-boy persona he wore so well. It made him seem benign, unthreatening, unremarkable. But I could see through it now to the intense stillness in his body and eyes that told of his strength and control.

"I only stopped by briefly to make sure you were all right. But your sister thinks it isn't safe for me to go out again, so I'll be staying the night," he said with an apologetic smile. "I'm sorry to intrude."

"You just happened to be strolling through the Frost after dark?" Jonn raised both eyebrows as if he couldn't believe it. He grabbed his crutches and hobbled forward to the door.

Adam met his gaze squarely. "Yes."

"Ivy, can you get some spare quilts for the floor?" I interrupted.

Jonn and Adam drew back as my sister passed between them to fetch the blankets. Adam went to the fire, and Jonn hobbled back for the bedroom. I stood in the middle of the room, my stomach twisting as I tried to think of a way to sooth my brother.

After she'd returned and we'd made a bed, Ivy peppered Adam with questions about village gossip while I went to help Jonn situate himself.

"What's he doing here?" he demanded quietly. "Is it...is it *their* business?"

He meant the Thorns. I knew he did.

"I want to talk to him about what happened to Edmond Dyer," I said. It was true enough.

He frowned, but we didn't continue the conversation because his tremors were starting. I covered him in quilts and laid a damp cloth over his eyes, and he fell asleep almost immediately.

After a moment of watching his chest rise and fall in even, quiet breaths, I rose and went out to the main room. Ivy had vanished, and Adam sat alone by the hearth, his legs drawn up to his chest and his face half in shadow. The firelight flickered over the points of his hair and turned the edges of his lashes to gold. He smelled like wood smoke and forest pine, and the scent had mingled with the smoky smell of the room, tuning my senses to his presence in a subtle but insistent way. I stopped in the doorway, leaning against it. He turned to face me, and for a moment the silence stretched and thickened between us.

"She went to bed," he said of Ivy, jerking his chin at the stairs.

I nodded but didn't speak.

Adam's eyes slid back to me, and he watched me with an intensity that made my stomach twist.

"I—I found them in the woods. They had a makeshift Thorns sign of twigs." I hesitated. "They're covered in cuts and bruises. The girl can't be a day older than ten. The boy is half her age."

Adam's jaw twitched. "The Aeralian government has sunk to new depths if they're arresting children."

"They didn't tell me anything," I said. "They didn't say anything, really."

"They're in shock."

Our eyes met again, and I took a deep breath. "And you'll take them to the gate yourself?"

"Tomorrow," he said. "At first light."

The air in the room seemed to grow thicker. I moved across the room and settled down by the hearth.

My eyes dropped to the quilts Ivy had brought, and I ran my hand over the top one.

"My mother made this for me," I said slowly, tracing the blue and white edges of the quilt with my forefinger. "It's a map of the whole Frost, made from bits of our old clothing and sewn together with our quota leftovers. She used to say it was the only time the Frost would keep me warm." My laugh stuck in my throat, and I grabbed some of the wool by Jonn's chair and began twisting it between my fingers. When in doubt, always work on quota.

"Your mother was a remarkable woman," Adam said quietly, still gazing at me steadily.

I nodded.

Silence fell between us, and it might have been companionable except for the undercurrent of unspoken things that set me on edge.

"Adam."

"Yes?"

"Some young people stopped me in the village a few days ago."

One of Adam's eyebrows rose. He picked up some of the wool from Jonn's basket and joined me in my work. His fingers were unusually long, and they deftly worked the material. I stopped, staring. "What are you doing?"

"Helping you." He kept twisting.

"Nobody does that," I said. "You don't help other families with their quota. It just isn't done." He knew this. There were other Weaver families in our village, but they did not share our burden. We each carried our quota load alone.

He tipped his head to one side. "Maybe if more people helped each other, then we'd have fewer problems with shortages and hunger. Some are overworked, some are underworked."

"Problems?" I asked, although I wasn't surprised.

"Half the village is struggling to meet their quota. The Elder families sew pillows and embroider sashes and call it quota. And some families work their fingers to the bone and neglect their own chores." He shook his head in disgust. "This Farther occupation has only exposed the problem, but it didn't create it. Things are not shared equally here, although we boast as much."

I flushed, shamed because he thought we couldn't handle our own quota but equally touched that he cared enough to lend a hand, even if it embarrassed me. "Adam," I said quietly. "It's fine, really."

"Let me help."

He looked determined, so I quit protesting. I watched silently a moment as he worked, and something in me prickled with curiosity. "I would never have taken you for someone who'd push for change."

"No? Why do you think I joined an organization like the Thorns, then?"

"Oh."

"So what about these villagers who stopped you?" he asked, pointedly steering the conversation away from himself.

I wet my lips with the tip of my tongue. "They called themselves the Blackcoats, and they said they were going to drive out the Farthers."

Adam laughed, low and disbelieving. "Are they insane?"

"Their plans seemed foolish, but after what happened to Edmond Dyer, I...I almost want to join them."

His hands went still. "And what's stopping you?"

The words I needed to say were crowded on my tongue. My chest constricted. This was important, and I wanted to make sure it came out right. I wasn't the kind of person who made lots of pretty speeches, but I wanted him to know exactly where I stood. "Well, their foolish ideas aside...they threatened Ann. They were blaming her for the Farther occupation and saying she needs to be taught a lesson."

He scowled. "Such misplaced fervor will get them nowhere. The Mayor's daughter is not to blame for the mistakes of the town."

I nodded. "But they had a point. People are being hurt. Terrible injustices are occurring...and nobody seems to be doing anything." Memories of the bruises on the children's bodies flashed through my mind.

He waited for me to continue.

"I can't join the Blackcoats, because I can't agree with their methods. But those children...Edmond Dyer's arrest...I must do something." I put down the wool and slid one hand into my pocket. As Adam watched, I reached out and uncurled my fingers. The brooch sat in the middle of my palm, glittering in the light of the fire.

"I want to join the Thorns."

The fire crackled, and the air seemed to buzz with the silence that followed. My fingers trembled, but I felt a strange exhilaration, too. I'd said it. I'd had the courage. A dizzying lightness filled me.

Adam spoke. "The goals of the Thorns are not necessarily the same as the goals of—"

"I know," I interrupted. "I know your prerogatives aren't necessarily mine. You're from beyond the Frost, and the Thorns are Aeralian, and I am a Frost dweller. But I think there's more at stake here than just my people's safety, Adam. Aeralians are people, too." I thought of Gabe. "But if what's happening here is wrong, then what's happening in Aeralis is just as wrong. My parents understood this. It's why they risked everything to help people. And I...I want to do the same thing."

"As long as you understand," he said, "the Thorns have bigger goals than the liberation of the Frost."

I held his gaze steadily. "I understand."

"It will be dangerous."

"I understand," I repeated.

"It will be difficult," he warned. "You will have difficult tasks to complete, secrets to keep."

Still, I held out the brooch.

"Well, then," he said, and a ghost of a smile graced his lips. He put his hand over mine, and his fingers were warm as he closed my hand around the brooch for the second time. "Welcome to the cause."

~

I lay in bed, drifting in the gray area between sleep and wakefulness, listening to Ivy's steady breathing and straining for the scrape of claws against the walls again even in my dreams. True rest was impossible. The air was too dark, too close, too stifling. The night was too silent. An ache of unspoken emotion squeezed me like a band of rope tied too tight—half excitement, half terror.

My chest rose and fell with uneven breaths as I twisted beneath the sheets. The presence of the Watchers brought back memories of my parents' deaths, and the fugitives in my barn made me think of Gabe.

Gabe...

My chest squeezed with sudden pain as I pictured his face.

I rolled over on my side and shut my eyes. Fatigue clung to my eyelids like grit, but my thoughts squirmed and scrabbled in my head, refusing to let me rest.

A heavy silence blanketed the house. Adam slept below by the fire, and Jonn slept in my parents' old bed. It might have been mine and Ivy's after my parents died, since there were two of us and only one of him, but I liked sleeping upstairs in the loft. I usually felt as secure as a bird tucked in a nest high above the forest floor, but tonight any illusions of safety eluded me. We were more like rabbits in a cage here in this farmhouse, surrounded by the snow and wind and forest and Watchers pawing at the sides. The Frost had us all by the throat, its icy fingers choking tighter and tighter. Now the Farthers were squeezing, too. Someday, maybe one of them would succeed in killing us all.

These morbid thoughts kept me company until the bluish glow of dawn began to leak through the curtains. I threw off the quilt and dressed quickly, pulling on my thick undergarments and then my ragged woolen dress. As I dug into the top drawer of my bureau, my fingers brushed the Thorns brooch. A shiver of icy anticipation passed over me. I pushed it back behind a pile of socks and shut the drawer.

Downstairs, the floorboards creaked, and the faintest squeak of a shoe met my ears. I hurried to the stairs and tiptoed down them, careful to not wake my sister. But when I reached the bottom, the room was empty. A brown leather cuff etched with a snow blossom lay on my chair.

I grabbed the cuff and ran to the door. I wrenched it open. Pale light poured over me.

He was already halfway across the yard, heading for the barn. His cloak fluttered in the wind, and his footprints scarred the freshly fallen whiteness.

"Adam!"

He heard me and turned.

I shoved my feet into my boots and went out into the yard without my cloak. The snow brushing my face like wet feathers had already half-filled the Watcher tracks that circled the house, and the lantern still burned at the edge of the woods, the light casting a halo amid the snowfall and the gloom of daybreak.

I ran. When I reached him, I held up the cuff. "You forgot this." I was breathless.

He watched my face carefully. "It's for you."

"Oh." I dropped my eyes to the leather bracelet, turning it over and over in my hands. It was smaller than his, and daintier. I was startled by the gift, and touched. I didn't know what to think or say. "It's beautiful. Thank you."

And it was. Delicate tooling lined the edges, and the snow blossom adorning the middle was the pale blue of a morning sky. I traced the painted petals with one finger and felt Adam's gaze lingering on my face.

"There's a reason beyond vanity for wearing it," he said, faintly amused. "I've discovered drawings work better than the real thing at warding Watchers away."

"I should embroider one on the back of my cloak, then," I muttered.

Adam looked thoughtful. "Not a bad idea. Wear the cuff, though. You'll be safer when you venture out in the darkness. I make sure my own are protected."

"Venture out in the...darkness?" Was he expecting me to have his boldness, to go out alone in the night?

"I was going to leave you a note in the barn," he said. "I must go, but we need to speak further about the Thorns. Think of this as your first assignment. A test."

My stomach squeezed at the words *first assignment*. I waited for him to continue. Snow fell around us, and I realized how cold I was without my cloak.

"You have to be sworn in, taught the rules," he said. "Joining isn't as simple as saying it."

"I know," I said.

He didn't smile, but I saw faint amusement in his eyes at my impatience. "Meet me tomorrow at dawn.

Follow the path to the charred oak and then go fifty paces. I'll meet you under the stingweed."

"Under the stingweed?"

"It's a test," he repeated. "I want to see if you can figure it out."

"Adam—" There was so much I didn't understand still.

His eyes softened slightly. "Until then, remember the signal. I will keep in touch, sometimes by note. It is our main method, although it can be exploited, so be watchful. I'll always transcribe mine with the blossom."

I thought of my parents. They'd been betrayed by such a note, when Cole had lured them out into the Frost. I shivered. "I'll always look for it."

He smiled faintly. "Be safe, Lia Weaver."

I watched him slip into the barn for the children, and then I returned to the house before my siblings awoke.

SEVEN

THE SACK FILLED with our quota of yarn thumped against my knee as I hurried down the path for the village. The sun speared the forest around me with beams of dazzling sunlight, banishing the memories of the night before—the Farther children. The Watchers. Adam. Joining the Thorns.

It all felt so unreal.

I hadn't said anything to Ivy or Jonn yet, and the familiar rat of apprehension gnawed at my stomach. Would they be angry? Or would they support my wishes to follow in our parents' footsteps on such a dangerous path? I'd been quiet to the point of near silence at breakfast, but they'd probably interpreted my reticence to speak as reluctance to take the quota into the village or leftover turmoil from the night before. And I'd let them think whatever they wanted—my mind was reeling, my stomach was twisted in a dozen knots, my fingers shook as I fumbled with my cloak strings. I was still in an emotional snarl myself, and I had to sort it out in my own head first before I could even think of explaining anything to them.

The sunlight playing over the snow turned the path ahead into a diamond-encrusted road. Bluewings swooped and fluttered overhead in the bare branches of the trees, and a tiny part of me danced too, because a tiny part of me had ignited with hope. If the Thorns succeeded in driving out the Farthers, the Frost would be ours again.

Gabe's name took shape in my thoughts, but I pushed it away. Even if the Farthers left, he wouldn't be able to come back. He'd gone through the portal. He was gone, and the ache I felt whenever I thought about it made it hard to breathe.

I rounded the curve in the path, and the Farther soldiers swung into sight. Was it just my imagination, or were there even more of them than before?

Steeling myself with a deep breath, I hurried again for the gate to the village.

Ann waited for me in the town square, her cloak and hood standing out in a shock of red color against the grays and browns and blues around her. When she spotted me, her eyes fluttered closed, and she pressed a hand to her mouth.

"You're all right," she gasped as soon as I'd reached her. She grabbed me and hugged me hard.

"What's wrong?" I said, pushing her back so I could peer into her face. "What is it?"

"Three men are missing, and they think Watchers..." She grabbed my hands as if she had to be sure I was real. "Your farm is out there all alone, without walls or weapons, and when you were running late for the quota delivery, I was afraid you weren't coming. Ever."

Dread spread through me. "Men are missing? Who?"

There hadn't been a Watcher-caused death since Cole. Sometimes a bear got some unsuspecting Hunter, or a snow panther sprang on a Trapper when he wasn't vigilant. But Watchers... Usually we were more careful. But it happened, and every time it did our smiles grew a little thinner and we drew our cloaks a little tighter.

"Two Fishers and a Farther soldier. The men were out after dark bringing in extra fish for the soldiers, and the Farther soldier was overseeing their work so they wouldn't take any for themselves."

Fishers. They usually kept to themselves, living at the edges of the village or in the forest, preferring to spend most of their time along the black waters of the river or on the ice that covered the lake. Like any forest-traveling Frost dweller, they knew the risks and shouldn't have lost their lives, but thanks to the Farthers... I couldn't speak at first, I was so incensed. Then another thought washed over me. If I hadn't insisted Adam stay the night, he might be missing, too. I felt ill. "And their families...?"

"They've organized search parties, but everyone knows they aren't going to find anything," Ann continued in a hushed voice. "So people are already gathering with the families to mourn. They've even moved quota to tomorrow, because everyone has been in such turmoil and half the men are searching the woods."

Nobody held on to hope long when it came to those who went missing in the forest. If the Watchers didn't kill them, the cold would. A night of exposure was all it took in our harsh world.

I scanned the streets around us. White-faced people whispered in doorways and hurried past with their cloaks pulled tight around their shoulders. The soldiers on the corner were smoking, and the ends of the cigs glowed like tiny fires.

"What have the soldiers done about it? Officer Raine? Aren't they supposed to be protecting us?" Derision dripped from my voice.

She took a deep breath. "He's furious, of course. He's insinuating that the whole thing might be our fault."

"Our fault?" I demanded. "He can thank himself for stirring up the Watchers. How does he think he can pin this on us?"

"Well," she said, "let me show you."

I followed her across the street to quota yard, where she stopped before the gate and pointed. My mouth fell open.

An angry torrent of painted words streaked across the far wall like a splatter of gore.

This is what happens when you try to conquer the Frost.

And

Farthers beware...the monsters like the taste of your blood.

And

Don't go out after dark, Mayor.

The ugly sentiments made my stomach curl and my hands shake. People were dead. The Frost was dangerous. But this...this disgusted me. And they mentioned the Mayor... I looked at Ann. She was wide-eyed, white-faced, absorbing it with me.

"Have you heard of the group calling itself the Blackcoats?" she whispered.

My stomach dropped like a stone. Did I dare tell her they'd tried to recruit me against her? "I...I've heard of them."

"They're a group who say they oppose the Farther occupation—violently if they have to. They hate my father. And apparently, they've taken this incident as an opportunity to threaten Raine."

"And your father." I stared hard at the letters again, the way the paint dripped like black blood, the way the R in *Mayor* smeared sideways against the stone, as if the vandal scrawling it had been interrupted and forced to flee.

She grabbed my arm and tugged me gently away from the yard and its bold-faced defacement. "I'll be all right. It's Raine we should be worried about, not these vandals."

I tugged at the scarf around my neck as my blood boiled with anger. Was Leon insane, making such a bold and stupid gesture? He might as well have spit in Raine's face. "Are you sure?"

"I'm sure." She scanned the streets, chewing at her lip. She seemed uneasy despite her reassuring words. "Let's go to my house—our cook made too much food last night. I thought you could make use of the leftovers."

My cheeks burned, but I was not too proud to refuse charity when we needed the food. "All right."

We reached the top of the hill out of breath and took a path through the snow-filled garden to the back door. Ann slipped off her red cloak and hood, and I removed my shabby one.

"Raine's here," she warned. "So we must be quick. You wouldn't want to run into him today."

We stepped into the kitchen. The cook glanced at us and then away with the practiced expression of disinterest that the staff of a wealthy family was always so good at affecting.

Ann went to the cupboard and took out a basket. "Here," she said. "Lots of day-old bread, and pastries, and a little smoked fish."

A voice echoed through the door. My skin prickled as I recognized it.

Officer Raine.

Ann's eyes met mine, and a shiver ran down my spine as I saw the calm and quiet despair in her gaze. She made no effort to shield me from the angry words filtering through the door. She simply handed me the basket, and then we both stood without speaking, listening.

"...Tear this disgusting little smear of a town apart until we find the vandals responsible for those messages!"

A quiet, unintelligible murmur—the Mayor's voice.

"I don't care if you have to arrest every single villager!"

Another murmur.

"...Then I will make them talk!" His voice dropped to a dangerous purr, but I could still hear him clearly through the door. "If I find out any person in this village has been helping *anyone* who opposes me, I'll hang them from the highest tree in the Frost. Do you understand?"

The Mayor didn't reply. The kitchen hummed with silence. My stomach plummeted to my toes as the words echoed in my mind. Sweat broke out across my palms, and my heart hammered.

He would kill me if he knew what I was.

I stole a glance at the cook. Her plump shoulders stooped as she bent over the sink, scrubbing a dish. Tendrils of hair stuck to her damp neck. She gave no indication that she heard anything.

"Perhaps you should get home," Ann said quietly, observing the expression on my face. I nodded.

I'd heard all I wanted to hear.

~

The falling snow from the night before had almost completely erased the evidence of the Watchers in the yard and around the farmhouse. Bathed in white, the house looked pristine, almost tranquil. Snow was redemptive like that—it smoothed away the flaws and painted everything in a clean coat of white, and it made the world seem new and beautiful again no matter how bad the night before. Perhaps that was how we survived in a place like the Frost. We let the snow bathe the tragedy away and moved on with our lives as if it hadn't happened.

The snow might cover tracks in the snow, but I couldn't as easily remove the memories in my mind. Avoiding the house, I stopped at the barn to give myself time to gather my thoughts and emotions. I completed the chores methodically, my mind scattered in a thousand pieces as my hands brushed the horses and fed the chickens. Adam, the Watchers, the Farthers, Ann, Everiss, Jonn, and Ivy...I was too connected, too distracted by my loyalties. It broke all the rules I used to follow.

But what else could I do?

I found the note pinned against the wall of the barn as I exited it, the paper fluttering in the wind like a captured butterfly. I plucked the scrap of white from the wall and smoothed it against my palm to read it.

The words scrawled across the paper made my heart freeze and then thud in staccato:

Those who aren't with us are against us, and there are more dangers than Watchers in the Frost.

It was from the Blackcoats. I was sure of it.

My hands shook as I put the note in my pocket and tried to think. Someone had been prowling around the farm. Leon? That toothy-grinned girl, Onna? I hadn't noticed any footprints on the path, but of course the snow had fallen and covered everything. Anyone could have come and gone.

I finished the rest of the chores and returned to the house. Ivy and Jonn looked up from the fire as I put away the food Ann had given me and returned to the main room. I smoothed my face into a mask of careful indifference and told them about the missing men.

They didn't say much—what was there to say? People died here. It was what happened.

We did not speak much as we worked, and the crackle of the fire on the hearth punctuated the silence.

Finally, my brother cleared his throat. "How is Everiss Dyer's family coping with the arrest of their father? Did you see them in town?"

"I didn't ask. I'll be sure to ask Ann when I go back tomorrow. I have to take the quota."

His gaze lingered on my face, as if he were looking for something else behind my eyes. I blinked and glanced away. I had no plans to tell them about the note. Those threatening words had been intended for me, and me only. The Blackcoats had no quarrel with Jonn and Ivy, and they were already worried enough about Raine and the Farthers.

A pang of terror struck me. Had Ivy gone to do the chores earlier? Had she seen the note?

I scrutinized them both as they returned to their work. Ivy's face seemed clear of duplicity, and I knew how bad my sister was at hiding her feelings, so I was reassured.

She muttered to herself as she twisted the thread with her thumb and forefinger, oblivious to me.

"Any other news from the village?" Jonn asked.

I thought about the way Ann's eyes shifted from mine these days, the scratch on her cheek. I thought of the words painted on the quota wall, the brewing animosity between the villagers, and the things Raine had shouted.

But all these things would only make them worry.

"No," I said.

~

I lay in bed while the snow fell outside and the house creaked and settled in its sockets around me. I traced Gabe's bracelet with my fingers and thought about the missing Fishers. My mind kept playing back the night we'd taken Gabe to the gate. The guttural growl from the shadows. The jaws that came out of nowhere. The red stain left on the snow.

And now I was supposed to venture out into the darkness to meet Adam?

I tried to sleep, but every time I shut my eyes I saw red on the snow.

The hours trickled by like melting icicles, and my thoughts chased in circles. My parents. Gabe. I tried to think about them, but the memories of their faces eluded me. Panic flooded my veins, and I focused on breathing slowly. I did not care for them any less if I couldn't remember the colors of their eyes, I told myself.

But the sick feeling in my stomach wouldn't go away.

I had to go to meet Adam. It was a test, he'd said. A test of cleverness, a test of mettle, a test of bravery. He wanted to see if I had what it took. It wasn't a matter of safety. The Watchers would be gone by then.

Wouldn't they?

In that window of time between night and day, no one really knew.

I lifted one damp hand to brush strands of hair from my eyes. My fingers trembled, and I stared at them in the near-blackness a moment. Sitting up, I reached for my bureau drawer. My hands found the cuff Adam had given me, and I slipped it onto my wrist. Instantly I felt safer.

Shutting my eyes, I didn't open them again until dawn.

EIGHT

I CREPT DOWN the stairs from my bedroom slowly, stepping around all the places I knew would squeak. I paused a moment and listened in the darkness for any sound to indicate my siblings had heard my descent and awoken, but all was still. The familiar hush of fallen snow wrapped the house in a thick silence and muffled all sound from outside. Inside, the darkness breathed with the faint creaks and groans of boards settling against the cold, and I could hear the wheezing sound of my sister snoring.

Otherwise, all was quiet.

I tiptoed on, pausing at the door to wrestle into my boots and wrap my cloak around my shoulders. I tied a string of snow blossoms around my neck, gathered up the lantern, and drew open the front door. A blast of chilly wind rushed over my cheeks and stole my breath. Casting one last glance over my shoulder at the warm darkness behind me, I stepped onto the porch and pulled the door shut.

Snow and shadow swathed the outside world, and light tinged the horizon even though the sun had not yet risen. Mist painted the barn in shades of gray, and the forest beyond made a black wall encircling the farmyard. Above my head, the Watcher Ward clattered in the wind. I could smell and taste the cold as I faced the woods.

The world was still dark. The Watchers still roamed somewhere in the shadows of the deep forests. My skin crawled with awareness of each gust of wind and scrape of branches against each other.

I didn't want to do this, but Adam was waiting. This was my moment to prove myself.

I struck a match and lit the lantern. The flame flared to life, and I half-closed the shutters to restrict the light. Gathering in a lungful of frosty air, I wrapped my cloak tighter around my body and crossed the yard.

Each step seemed loud as a shout. The forest loomed closer and closer until I could smell the sharp scent of pine. My ears were tuned for any sound in the depths that might signal the approach of a Watcher, but I heard nothing. The shadows lay still. The trees made stark lines against the sky.

I kept moving. My lungs felt as unyielding as glass as I struggled to draw a quiet breath.

Another step, and another, and then the yard fell away as the trees crowded around me. The shadows enveloped me, and chills skittered over my skin.

I was in the Frost.

The light of almost-morning leaked silvery glints across the snow. The snow blossoms lining the path looked luminous, their petals glowing bright blue in the faint light. The snow sparkled, a dance of diamonds lit by stars.

I'd never been in the forest so early. I didn't recognize this terrible and beautiful fairy land.

A branch snapped behind me. I whirled, my hand going to the knife at my waist.

A pale white deer went loping away in the darkness, her tail flapping.

Lightheadedness swept over me. Just a deer.

I sucked in a breath and pressed on.

Follow the path until the charred oak, he'd said. So I hugged the edges of the road, brushing past the snow blossoms forming a tenuous line of safety between me and the deep forest. My eyes searched the line of trees for the oak. I knew the one he meant. It had been struck by lightning when I was a girl, and now the trunk grew twisted and strange.

All around me, the darkness hung heavy as a curtain.

I breathed a sharp sigh when I spotted the blackened trunk rising up from the forest around it like a half-desiccated corpse. I turned left, leaving the path and forging directly into the Frost. I counted the paces in my head as I moved until I reached a clearing. Trees made a wall around me, their scabby trunks slick with ice and dark with damp. I could smell the sharp scent of ice and pine. Above my head, the sky was a dark indigo laced with pink. No house or hut or other structure was in sight, and nothing in the darkness so much as moved.

The ground was damp and muddy from melted snow, and frost ferns covered the forest floor. If Adam was here, I couldn't see where.

Where was I supposed to go now?

Beneath the stingweed.

I spotted an abundance of the thorny bushes at the edge of the clearing. Stubby branches of reddish-green poisoned nettles waved gently in the wind.

Beneath?

Crouching, I peered at the dark patch of earth underneath the curling branches of the stingweed. I could just barely make out the seam of wood against it.

A door, just like the one in the barn.

I set the lantern down and looked over my shoulder at the forest behind me. No red Watcher eyes glowed in the darkness, no Farthers lurked behind the trees. But the shadows shifted faintly, and my skin still crawled with apprehension. I bent back over the door, taking care not to brush against the stingweed branches.

My fingers found the handle after a moment of brushing over the ground. I tugged, and the door slid sideways, revealing a cavernous hole. The scent of mud and dampness rushed up at me.

I didn't dare call out for Adam. I thrust my foot inside and found a ladder bolted against the wall of the shaft. Grabbing the lantern, I opened the shutters so it gave a little light, and then I began to descend.

The lantern cast a pale yellow glow across the stone and dirt surrounding me. The hole was narrow, almost like a well and my sleeves brushed the sides as I climbed. Above me, the Frost was just an indigo circle against the blackness.

The suffocating sensation of being trapped pressed against my throat like invisible fingers, but I fought the panic down and kept climbing. I was almost there.

Finally, mercifully, my feet touched dirt. I stepped down from the ladder and turned toward the scent of musky air that wafted toward me, betraying some further hollowness ahead.

"Hello?" My voice echoed faintly up the tunnel I'd just descended.

The scuff of a footstep made my hair prickle. I lifted the lantern and fumbled for my knife.

The shadows stirred and formed a human shape. "You made it," a voice said quietly.

My heartbeat slowed a little as I recognized him. "Adam."

I stepped away from the ladder, and the light from my lantern illuminated the space—walls of stone and earth, shelves stuffed with books, a rug thrown over a dirt floor. Several black boxes sat on a desk, and I wanted to ask what they were, but I didn't dare.

The light illuminated his face. "Any sign of Watchers on your way here? Any glimpse of tracks?"

He must have heard about the missing men. Had he worried about me arriving unscathed? I couldn't tell from his expression.

"None," I answered, trying to look as unaffected as possible. I allowed myself to glance around at the shadowed corners, the boxes, the dark earthen ceiling and walls. "What is this place?"

"A Thorns meeting place much like the one beneath your barn," he said, still watching me as if looking for signs of stress or fear.

"It seems...old."

"They were built long ago. We've only adopted them for our use. It is secret, so do not reveal it to anyone else."

"I won't."

The lantern light steeped his face in shadow, making inky pools of his eyes, and it was hard to read his gaze. The intensity in it made me shiver.

"There isn't much time," he said, "and I want to keep this brief. Do you swear to follow the orders of your superiors, risk life and limb for the cause of the Thorns, and keep your mouth shut about your secret activities?"

I choked on a laugh. "Is that really the official oath?"

His mouth quirked in a faint smile. "No. But it's very long, and out here in the Frost we skip most of the formalities."

"I swear it," I said. "Wait. Who are my superiors?"

"You should probably ask questions before swearing to things," Adam said dryly, turning his head to hide another smile. "As to your question, your immediate superior is me."

"Were you my parents' superior, too?"

"I was."

A shiver went through me, a little skitter of feeling that left quiet assurance in its wake. I was literally taking my parents' place.

"Any more questions?"

I had a thousand questions.

"How many operatives are in the Frost? Is your entire family involved?" I remembered his brother, Abel, joining us the night we took Gabe to the gate.

"That," he said, "is not your concern. We are not aware of all the others who might be Thorns operatives for purposes of security. That way, if you are caught and tortured, you cannot give away a list of names even if you want to. You know your immediate superior and any operatives below you, should you ever be in that position."

Tortured. I swallowed hard, my throat suddenly dry. "Does...does it happen a lot? Being caught and tortured, I mean."

Adam tipped his head to one side as if he were considering whether he wanted to reassure or frighten me with his answer. "Not a lot," he said finally.

I failed to feel too reassured, however. Officer Raine's words ran through my mind again. With him, there'd be no torture. Just swift, merciless execution.

I swallowed to ease my suddenly dry throat and pushed on to other thoughts, other questions.

"Will there be many fugitives?" In my mind's eye I saw the Aeralian children, so thin and bruised.

"Some," he said. "The ones who make it this far."

"Did they—are they—?" Hope rose in me, wild and unbidden.

"I sent them through the gate," he said. "They are safe."

Safe. Just as I'd promised them. I exhaled as an invisible weight slipped off my shoulders, and my mouth curved in a smile that quickly faded. "Will they be all right where they've gone?"

"There are many others who went before them," he said patiently. "They all go to the same place. The children will be cared for."

I nodded. Other questions begged to be asked, but I didn't know how to phrase them. "Where they go, is it...is it nice?"

Adam shook his head. "I don't know. I don't know where they go. The coordinates were fixed by someone else, and we dare not change them. Without the right coordinates, a traveler could fall off a cliff or into the ocean. They must be mapped carefully."

I shouldn't have expected that he would know. Why was I so disappointed? "And they..." I paused. "They can't come back, can they?"

He said it without emotion, but the words crushed me anyway. "To return requires a second working gate. There is only one still in existence, the one hidden in the deep Frost and guarded by the Watchers."

Breathing was suddenly impossible. I already knew this, somehow, but hearing the fact spoken so plainly was like being punched in the stomach. I struggled to keep my face expressionless even as my pain spiked through my chest. "I understand."

"Any other questions?" His voice was gentler this time, as if he could see my pain.

I shook my head and took a deep breath. Life went on. It always went on. That was the way of the Frost.

It should be my way, too.

"What about the Farthers in the village?" I managed. "What about Raine?" Then I told him about the messages the Blackcoats had left on the walls, and the note they'd left for me. Adam listened in silence with a frown of concentration. When I'd finished, he got up and paced.

"We have a very important task right now, one that will draw us away from the village. For now, simply try to lie low and avoid drawing any attention to yourself when it comes to Raine and his soldiers. The Blackcoats may dig their own grave, but we do not have to be mixed up in that."

A very important task?

But light was beginning to trickle down the ladder and into the room, bathing us in gray and pink and banishing the shadows. Adam went to the well and peered up, gauging the time. "Keep your eyes and ears open in the village, of course. If you ever need to contact me, use the lantern signal as you've been doing and leave a message buried beneath it. Come here only in a moment of complete necessity—this location is secret. And prepare yourself. I am going to need your help."

"When?" Fear and excitement fizzled in my chest.

"Tomorrow. I'll meet you in the late afternoon. We'll need the horses. I'll be behind the barn at the time you normally do your evening chores, waiting for you."

If we needed the horses, then we were going deep into the Frost. Nervousness prickled me, but I held my tongue. I knew he wouldn't tell me more, and I wanted to prove I could follow orders without demanding answers at every turn.

I climbed back up the ladder, and Adam followed with the lantern. When I reached the top, I dragged myself out with my forearms and climbed to my feet. I scanned the woods for any signs of Watchers. Nothing. The forest had turned gray, and pink streaked the sky. The icy terror that flavored the night had faded to the quiet ominousness of day.

"I'll see you soon, Lia Weaver," he said.

NINE

I STEPPED INSIDE the farmhouse and hung my cloak on the hook. A sigh slipped from my lips as I chaffed my frozen fingers together and stepped toward the kitchen. I'd done it. I'd survived the Frost alone in the dark and proved I was brave enough to be a part of the Thorns. Now I just needed to make some tea and warm myself up before Jonn and Ivy woke—

"*Lia.*"

My sister's voice cut through the air like a whip.

I spun on my heel and came face to face with my little Ivy. She stood in the entrance to the great room, her arms crossed over her chest and her fingers tapping against her elbows.

"You're awake," I said, trying to sound nonchalant as I smoothed down my wet clothes and cleared my throat. "I just came in. Are you hungry?"

"We know you didn't just get back from the barn."

"What?"

I lifted my gaze from Ivy's livid expression and saw Jonn sitting in his chair by the fire, his somber face in profile. The flames flickered over his forehead and freckled cheeks and made his red-brown hair gleam. When he turned his head, I saw his disappointment clearly in his eyes, but he didn't speak. For once, he just sat there as Ivy railed.

"Yes. We know you went out," my sister yelled. "How could you?"

"Ivy—"

"How could you get involved without telling us? How could you keep this a secret?"

"Ivy," I said again, louder this time, "you may not understand now, but—"

"The Blackcoats would accept us all, Lia, and you know it."

Blackcoats? I froze, and my voice dropped to a harsh whisper. "How do you know about them? Who have you been talking to?"

She blinked. The anger in my voice seemed to have startled her, and suddenly she was defensive and uncertain as she stammered a reply. "I've heard things in the village. People are whispering. They're going to free us. And—and I want to help, too."

"I'm not helping the Blackcoats," I said firmly. "I don't agree with their ideas or their methods."

"They're fighting for our freedom!"

"Ivy," I snapped. "They want to hurt Ann, and they would have wanted to hurt Gabe. They hate all Farthers, not just the ones like Officer Raine, and I can't accept that. I can't work with them. And that's all I want to say about it."

"But..."

"They threatened me. They *left us a threatening note*," I said.

Her mouth clamped shut at that. Jonn straightened. "What note?"

"Never mind," I said. "Forget it."

Ivy looked from me to Jonn, who was staring at me with a look of silent fury. "If you aren't working with the Blackcoats...?"

"It's the Thorns," he said quietly, speaking for me.

"Like Ma and Da," I said, desperate for them to understand. "I know it's dangerous, but I have to do this. There were children in the woods yesterday, fugitives from Aeralis. I can't turn these people away. I just can't."

"We know that, silly," she said. "Of course you have to do this. Of course we have to help them. So do we."

"No," I said sharply. I thought of Raine and the words I'd overheard him screaming at Ann's house. *If I find out any person in this village has been helping anyone who opposes me, I'll hang them from the highest tree in the Frost. Do you understand?* "It's too dangerous. Only I can do this."

Jonn shook his head at me. Our gazes held, and I felt the ache of his disappointment knife through me. But I wasn't going to back down. This was not a game. This was life and death.

"Lia?" Ivy snapped. "I want to join the Thorns, too."

"Don't be absurd," I said, still holding Jonn's gaze and trying to communicate the necessity of what I must do alone to him. "You're a child."

"I'm fourteen," she said. "Close to fifteen. I'm ready!"

"Absolutely not," I said.

"Lia's right," my brother said, surprising me with his show of solidarity. "You're too young." Then he pinned me with another look.

His meaning was clear. We were the same age.

"Jonn," I said, exasperated, "how are you supposed to help me if you can't walk more than two steps?"

His expression didn't change, but I saw the light in his eyes wither and immediately I hated myself. "I—I'm sorry. I didn't mean that."

He picked up a ball of half-rolled yarn from the basket by the fire and began winding it around his hand, and I felt the breech between us like a knife.

"Ivy," I said without looking at her, "please go milk the cow. I haven't done it yet."

"I don't—"

"Ivy."

She went, slamming the door behind her.

The air in the room felt too hot. Jonn wouldn't look at me. I crossed the floor to stand in front of him, but he kept winding the yarn, methodical in his movements.

"I didn't mean it."

He laughed, low and bitter. "Yes, you did."

"It came out wrong."

"You said what you meant."

A headache began to creep up the back of my skull. My voice was somewhere between a sigh and a plea. "You have to understand. What I'm doing is very dangerous. There's no way Ivy can do this."

He tipped his head to the side, his lips pulling down in a scowl. "Of course not," he said. "She's too little, like we both said. But *I* could help you."

I rubbed my hands over my eyes with a groan. I wasn't going to allow him to risk himself. "This isn't about playing music or telling riddles. This is life or death, and—"

"You didn't even tell me about that threatening note you got."

"Jonn..."

"Forget it." He yanked at the yarn in a rare show of frustration. I flinched.

"Let's not—"

"I said forget it."

I stood there another moment, my hands dangling uselessly at my sides and my mouth full of words that suddenly felt sharp and hurtful and ugly no matter how true they might be. Fighting with him felt wrong, like an ill-fitting garment that I'd put on by mistake. Usually we were so in sync, bound together by blood and friendship.

I strode to the door and yanked it open. My brother didn't turn or speak as I went out into the snow.

~

My sister was dumping a bucket of water into the horses' trough when I entered the barn. She didn't look up.

"Ivy?"

"I just want to help," she muttered without turning around. "And if you tell me I can help by working on quota, so help me..."

I leaned against the stall door beside her and put my hand on her arm. I tried to say it the way our mother would—sort of soft and gentle, but firm at the same time. "Please, Ivy. Try to understand."

She spun away from me. "You were mean to Jonn."

"I wasn't trying to be."

She stormed out, slamming the barn door behind her, and the silence felt empty after she'd gone.

I sighed and stared helplessly at the barn around me, and then I trudged back to the house. I had to take the quota into the village.

~

The villagers milled about with the quota, but everyone was quiet. The missing men had not been recovered.

I looked at the wall where the message had been written, but fresh whitewash covered the spot. I bit my lip.

"Lia," Ann said from behind me, and I slowed so she could catch up.

"The men still haven't been found?"

"No," Ann whispered. "And Raine is furious. He is blaming the village. He says he wants to know who wrote the message on the wall, but no one will come forward or name any names."

If he got any names, those people would be killed. I shuddered.

A Farther soldier's gaze slid over us as we entered the quota yard and joined the end of the long line, and I shivered under his scrutiny. Were they looking for members of the Blackcoats? After a moment, he averted his gaze. I let out my breath slowly. Beside me, Ann's shoulders relaxed slightly, as if she'd found the soldier's gaze just as nerve-racking.

The line crept forward a few inches as another villager received his allotment of salt, sugar, and other foodstuffs, and then scurried home. Ann and I shuffled forward with the rest.

"How are Everiss and her family?" I kept my voice low as I eyed the Farther soldier standing guard beside the quota master. What did the Farthers think we were going to do, riot? These little shows of power disgusted me almost as much as they frightened me.

Ann didn't immediately reply. She seemed deep in thought, her eyes unfocused and her lips pressed together tightly. I nudged her, and she sighed, blinked, and gave me a tight little smile she'd learned from her father. "Another family took them in temporarily, although I don't know what they'll do. She has three younger sisters. But she won't say much to me or anyone. She's been keeping to herself. I heard the soldiers have been harassing her."

"What happened to their home?"

Ann looked away. "Officer Raine uses it now. The Dyers were nicely situated."

The pieces fell into place. A manufactured story for a land grab. I bit my lip to keep from shouting, and I tasted blood. Ann put a hand on my arm.

"Don't," she whispered. "It won't help anything if you make a scene."

I shivered with rage, but stayed silent.

My gaze cut to the soldier standing at the front of the line again. He was thin and sharp-faced, and his expression was mask-like as he stared at the villagers stepping past him to receive supplies. If I hadn't already known other Farthers, kind ones like Gabe, I'd think every single one was a devil in human form.

The line moved again. We were almost to the front of the yard now, and the platform loomed before us. The soldier at the front leered at Ann. "Too bad your quota isn't keeping me company," he called out.

She ignored him, but two bright spots of color appeared on her cheeks. I simmered with silent rage, but Ann tugged me forward as the line moved again. I was next.

The quota master was fumbling with his list, looking for my name. I tapped my foot on the ground. If I didn't get out of here soon, I was going to explode.

"Girl," the soldier said again to Ann.

She turned her head as if checking the sky for signs of snow. The Farther soldier didn't like being ignored. He reached for Ann's sleeve.

I didn't think, I exploded. I swung a fist at his face.

"Lia!"

Ann grabbed my arm. My hand stopped an inch before the Farther's nose. The soldier drew his gun. The quota master was shouting something.

The soldier grabbed me by the shoulders and threw me to the ground.

I lay still, the icy dirt cutting into my cheek where I lay. My skin felt too hot, and my heart was pounding a call to war in my chest. My head ached from striking the ground.

Ann was speaking low and fast above me, but I couldn't make out the words. Out of the corner of my eye, I saw the soldier holster his weapon. Ann crouched and pulled me up.

"Just give the quota master your yarn and let's go," she said.

I looked at the soldier. His eyes bore into mine, and they promised violence. Grabbing my sack, I handed it to the quota master and accepted the supplies in return. Shame burned like a hot coal against my skin. My lungs hurt. I struggled to draw breath.

Ann put an arm around me and half-dragged me from the yard.

"What is wrong with you?" she demanded as soon as we'd stepped into the street. "Are you insane?" Blood flushed her cheeks and made her eyes feverishly bright. She grabbed my arms and shook me. "He could have hurt you."

"He tried to grab you!" I exploded.

"They're all talk."

"How dare these Farthers come into our town, harass our people, steal our land and our houses—"

"Lia," Ann said sharply. "Let it go. If you get angry, you'll become a target. You don't want that. Now come on, let's just go before he bothers us again." She turned toward the Assembly Hall.

I was rooted to the ground. My righteous anger blazed inside me like a white-hot flame. "So you're just going to do nothing? Sit back and let them stomp all over us like this?"

Ann's shoulders scrunched up, and she swung back around. Her eyes were two shards of blazing color in her white face. "What can I do? What can any of us do? They are bigger and stronger, and they have guns. We are *helpless* against them."

I let my breath out in a huff. I couldn't tell her anything about the Thorns, and the thought dug into me like Watcher claws. I wanted to scream with frustration.

"Come on," she said, softening. She grabbed my sleeve and tugged me down an alley between two stone shops with icicles hanging from their roofs. "You can't let them see you like this."

I took a deep breath. My frustration hissed in my veins like steam, but I struggled to suppress it. She was right. I had to be calm. What was happening to me? I used to be so unemotional, so strong and hard and ruthless in my decisions. Now I felt like a pot about to boil over, my emotions and feelings in constant turmoil, barely contained. Was this what love had done to me? Had my feelings for the Farther begun an infection of my emotions?

"I'm sorry," I breathed. "You're right. That was stupid of me."

"Very stupid," Ann agreed, but I heard the forgiveness in her voice.

"Ann? Lia?"

We both turned at the softly uttered exclamation and saw a girl with wispy brown curls and big gray eyes staring at us from the end of the alley. I recognized her— one of Everiss's younger sisters, Jullia. Her chapped, red fingers matched the skin around her eyes. A ragged scarf clung to her neck, the ends blowing in the wind, and she plucked at it nervously.

"Jullia," Ann said, giving me a quick glance that was clearly an order to compose myself. I swallowed hard and did my best to comply as we stepped forward, our feet crunching against the sludgy snow that lined the edges of the alley. Since when had Ann become the strong one?

Jullia searched our faces for any signs of condemnation, and when she found none, her shoulders relaxed. A tired smile hovered at the edges of her mouth but never quite landed. "It's good to see a familiar face," she said with a note of exhaustion in her tone.

We murmured answers to her questions, and I tried to act as though I hadn't noticed we were standing in an alley whispering.

"How's your father?" Ann asked.

Jullia's face crumpled. "He is still a prisoner." She pointed at the end of the alley. "We're staying with the Tanners temporarily. Ma goes to see the Elders every day, hoping to find some way to have him released."

Tannin racks filled the small courtyard behind her. A bubbling pot sat over a fire in the middle of the yard, steam spilling from the top. The liquid inside churned thick and dark as blood. The air smelled like charcoal and wet wool. A plume of smoke smudged the sky above our heads and blocked the sun.

"Dye?" I murmured aloud, surprised. With Edmond Dyer in prison, was his family still expected to keep the trade?

"We still have to make our quota if we want supplies," Jullia explained, noticing my look. "Even without Father here to help, the numbers haven't changed..." Her voice wobbled, and she looked away. When she turned her face back, her eyes were red but her face was composed. "It's hard," she finished.

My fingers knotted into fists. More injustice, this time from the Elders. They could hardly blame the Farthers for such tyranny. What was happening to our village? Had everyone gone mad?

Ann bit her lip as she took in the sight of the makeshift dye supplies and Jullia's exhausted expression. "Is Everiss here now?"

Jullia shook her head, and the curls that framed her cheeks shivered at the movement. "She's been sneaking away whenever she thinks I won't notice. I wonder if she's trying to see Father. None of us have been able to speak with him."

"No matter," Ann said carefully, although I didn't miss her surprise at the news that Everiss was missing. "I'll speak to her later."

I looked at the piles of yarn waiting to be dipped in color. Did Jullia have to do all this herself? "Can we help you?" I burst out.

The courtyard filled with silence. My own words to Adam echoed in my head. *You don't help other families with their quota. It just isn't done.*

"I have a few minutes," I said quickly. "I don't...I mean, I am no Dyer, of course, but..."

Jullia's eyes looked suspiciously wet, but she blinked a few times and managed to produce another weak smile. This time it lingered a few seconds. "Oh. Yes. Thank you."

Ann breathed in deeply. Her expression was briefly a startled one, as if I'd suggested we strip naked and paint ourselves blue, but then she nodded, too. "Of course. We have a few minutes to spare."

We worked quickly and clumsily under Jullia's direction, dipping the yarn into the steaming liquid using special forks. The yarn seeped up the color and turned a deep shade of red. Jullia hung the freshly dipped pieces against the side of the house, and the dye dripped into the snow below. In my head, I saw a flash of blood against the snow. I blinked the memory away.

By the time we'd finished, the sun had climbed high in the sky. The day was slipping away.

"I think we should be going," I said. "Ivy and Jonn might worry."

107

Jullia grabbed my hand with her purple-stained ones. She fumbled for words. "Thank you," she said finally, and her face crumpled as if she wished she could say more, but didn't know how to do it.

Ann hugged her, and we turned to go.

A sigh squeezed between my lips as we reached the road and I stretched. My shoulders ached and my back throbbed after an hour of dying. What must Jullia and Everiss feel like, doing this day after day? For the first time in my life, I was thankful to be a Weaver.

Neither of us commented on the fact that we'd helped Jullia. But I felt a little lighter. We'd helped her, even if it was against tradition. Maybe Adam was right.

"Oh, Lia," Ann said as we turned the corner. "They are living in squalor, fulfilling their quota in a dirty alley. There were *rats*."

"They have a lot more to worry about besides rats," I said, glancing down the street in search of Farther soldiers. Didn't she understand? They were completely and utterly vulnerable. They were being forced to fulfill their quota without the adequate resources or means to do so.

They were being broken. Punished.

Sharpness and shadow filled the village now, almost as much as the Frost outside. At least in the Frost, we had the snow blossoms to ward the Watchers off. Here, there was nothing to keep the Farthers at bay if they wanted to kill one of us, and the monsters in uniform roamed day and night.

Ann bit her lip. I looked at the sky—it was time for me to be heading back—and then at her face. "I've got to go."

She nodded.

I hovered there a moment, both reluctant and eager to leave. Worry tugged at my heart with invisible threads as I studied my friend's pale face. I didn't miss the way her eyes swept the street, or the way her fingers trembled.

What was she not telling me?

"Be safe," she said, her teeth bone-white against her lips as she tried to smile and failed. We touched hands, and I stepped away from her and down the street for the gate. When I looked over my shoulder, she had already vanished.

With unease gnawing at my gut, I turned my face toward home.

TEN

WHEN LATE AFTERNOON came, I saddled the horses, running my fingers over their shaggy coats to check for burrs before settling the blankets over their backs and then the saddles. When I retrieved the bridles, a shadow moved against the light of the window, and Adam was taking one of the bridles from my hand as I sucked in a startled breath. "You frightened me!"

"Sorry," he murmured, not looking remotely sorry. He took the bridle and slipped to the side of one of the horses, the taller one with a star on her forehead. He slid the bit into the horse's mouth, crooning softly to the animal as she tossed her head. He glanced at me. "What do you call this one?"

"Doesn't have a name." I approached the second horse, a gelding with four white socks.

Adam shot me a baffled look. "No name?"

"What point is there in naming them? They aren't pets."

"Do you always have such a dire view of things?"

"It's not dire," I protested. "It's sensible. When you name things, you start worrying about if the Watchers will get them, and if they'll be warm enough, and if they'll be taken away from you. You start to care."

He shook his head and reached up to rub the mare between her eyes affectionately. I remembered he was good with horses. "Star, then," he said, murmuring more words to the mare. She flicked one of her ears in his direction and nickered softly.

I scowled at him in mock annoyance. "You can't just name my horse."

"I thought they didn't belong to you. I thought you just boarded them here in exchange for extra supplies."

I couldn't argue with that kind of logic, unfortunately. I crossed my arms and did some more fake scowling.

Adam pointed at the gelding. "That one is Officer Raine."

A sly smile crossed my lips. "Well, just the back half of him."

Adam threw his head back and laughed in startled appreciation.

Still smiling, I led the gelding out into the snow. Adam followed with the mare, and we mounted them just outside the paddock behind the barn. We were hidden from the house, a fact that made me glad.

My smile faded as I faced the dark shadows of the forest. The wind caught my hair and ruffled my cloak, and a chill swept over my skin. Even in the light of day, the woods radiated danger.

I looked at Adam and found him watching me.

"Are you ready to go back?"

My heart stuttered in my chest. "Back?"

Instead of replying, he kicked his horse into a gallop and rode straight into the forest. I had no choice but to follow as he crossed the perimeter of the trees and plunged into the Frost.

The sunlight always looked different in the woods, all diluted and glowing, almost as if we were underwater. It was strange to forge ahead without a path to mark the way. The trees were just slashes of black and brown against the white drifts of snow, with

111

the occasional flash of red berries or the shock of blue where a snow blossom bush bloomed, and the prickly scent of pine mingled with the smell of damp bark and melting snow.

The horses snorted, the sound punctuating the eerie silence along with the stamp of their hooves in the snow. Still, a hush enveloped us, discouraging words. I exhaled softly, unable to shake the feeling that we were being watched. I turned in the saddle, scanning the trees for movement.

But the dark hollows were still, silent.

The horses moved swiftly, leaping over fallen trees and galloping up embankments. When we reached a hill, Adam drew the mare back to a walk and let my gelding catch up.

"Do you remember when we met in these woods several months ago?" he asked as he scanned the trees.

The image of him standing with his back to me, a cloaked figure amid all the white, was forever branded in my mind. One of the horses had run away—Star, in fact—and Gabe and I had followed her deep into the forest. We'd come upon Adam suddenly, and I had kissed Gabe to distract Adam from seeing his face and realizing he was not a villager. And it had worked. Adam hadn't realized who Gabe was. And then he'd given me a hint that led later to my discovery of the secret room filled with Thorns documents beneath the barn floor.

"I remember," I said quietly.

"I was looking for the gate. Since your parents' deaths I'd been searching the Frost for it. They had all the maps, all the knowledge. I was not privy to that information when they were alive."

"But you knew about the secret room beneath our barn. Why didn't you look there for the maps?"

He met my gaze. "I *did* look. They weren't complete. Don't you remember?"

"True," I said, surprised he'd stolen into our barn at some indeterminate point in the past without our knowing. But then I remembered the ease with which he'd slipped into the barn this afternoon, the way he moved through the Frost at night, almost as if by magic. "So you didn't find anything. You didn't know where it was."

"Half of the two maps needed to chart the way had been stolen. Your father often carried the second map with him. He was charting as he explored. We knew so little about the ancient ruins, and he was the expert. He must have dropped it in the Frost the day he died. At first I wasn't sure if you had found it, or someone else, and for a time I didn't dare approach you for fear of betraying myself as a Thorns operative to anyone who might be watching."

Thinking about my father's death made my throat squeeze and my eyes burn, but I hungered for these details, too. I took a deep breath and let it out. "Cole was watching, remember? He found the map and gave it to the Mayor, and I saw it when I went to confess about Gabe. I remembered it later when we found the maps, and I made a copy with Ann's help the same day I confronted you about working for the Thorns."

"Yes," Adam said. "You astonished me with your resourcefulness. I'd hoped I could start you on the path to uncovering your heritage with us, but I never dreamed you'd accomplish so much on your own."

His unexpected praise startled me. I bit my lip and stared at the mane of the horse instead of looking at him. Adam wasn't free with his compliments. It meant a lot, coming from him.

"Thank you."

"He was wrong about your parents," Adam said after another moment of silence.

I glanced up and found him gazing at me intently. His face was unreadable, his eyes clear and hard as flint. "He?"

"Cole," he said. "That night at the gate. He called them soft-hearted civilians. But they were a key part of the Thorns here. Their contributions were greater than most people realized."

The lump in my throat squeezed tighter. "Thank you," I whispered again. Their deaths had not been in vain, not if they'd done so much good.

"They were important players in the organization," he continued. "They gave their lives, and it wasn't for nothing. They saved the lives of hundreds with their efforts, perhaps more."

"Did many go through the gate?" I asked.

He mulled over his words, as if trying to choose the best way to put it. "Many did not make it this far. But some, yes."

Branches scraped at our faces and cloaks as we progressed farther into the Frost. Adam must have memorized the way, for he guided his horse with confidence around piles of rock and beneath sagging trees.

"How much longer?" I asked. I shot a wary glance at the late-afternoon sun.

"We're close," he said, pointing to the ground in front of us.

I caught my breath.

Watcher tracks—giant ones—marred the snow. The horses shied away, and I struggled to hold the gelding in place.

"They keep close to the gate," Adam said. "It's just up that hill."

My heart began to pound. But when we crested the top of the hill, I forgot my terror, because the scene before me took my breath away.

The trees fell away, and a swath of ice-crusted lake swept along the hill to our left. The mountains rose up in the distance, their peaks stabbing the storm clouds that hugged the horizon. Before us, the smooth curve of an icy beach glittered in the sunlight alongside the black waters of a lake. Everything was placid, peaceful...almost as if everything were sleeping.

"Is this...?" I looked around. Where were the ruined buildings? Where was the entrance? It seemed familiar, but only as if from a dream I'd had years and years ago and almost forgotten except for a faint, lingering impression.

Adam tipped his head. A grin teased across his lips. "You don't see it?"

"I..." I spurred my horse forward and rode toward the lake, craning my neck. I saw nothing but frozen ground and ice-covered rocks. I looked over my shoulder at Adam, who hadn't moved. Slowly, I turned the gelding around and galloped back to his side. "All right," I said. "You've had your fun. Where is it?"

He kicked the mare forward, riding straight for the mountains. I followed. He was crazy. He was riding toward nothing.

But then out of the corner of my eye, I caught the faintest glimmer of light, as if the sun were reflecting off metal. "Wha....?"

Suddenly, the whole world seemed to shift, and there it was.

I caught my breath.

The curve of the ruined buildings hugged the hills and gleamed in the sun. I blinked to make sure I wasn't imagining it this time. "How...? Where...? There was nothing there, and then suddenly there was." I was babbling now, but I didn't care. Was it magic?

"The ruins are shielded from sight during the day," Adam explained. "I rode past this very place when looking for the gate months ago and saw nothing. Some sort of ancient mechanism in place tricks the eye and makes it see nothing at all. I don't know how it works."

"We saw it that night when we brought Gabe," I protested. I drew a deep breath as the memories rushed over me in a waterfall of mental images. Cole, with a pistol in his hand. The dead Farther soldiers, their mangled bodies limp in the trampled snow. Gabe, his eyes on mine and his name on my lips. I gazed at the landscape.

Beneath this ground, he'd vanished in the blink of an eye.

"I've examined it several times since that trip. The shield dissipates at night, although I don't know the reason why," he said. "But that's when the Watchers guard it. So no one has ever found it here by accident."

"It's beautiful." Beautiful and strange. The smooth domes and arches hugged the ground and blended with the curves of the hills, almost as if their ancient makers had sought to hide them completely in the landscape. When I turned in the saddle to look behind us, the air was hazy, and the edges of the trees looked smudged. A shiver rippled over my skin.

Adam dismounted and led the mare to a cluster of small pines. He tethered her and then retrieved something from the bag hanging from his belt. I followed his lead and tethered the gelding. I dared ask the question that had been on my tongue for the last few hours. "What are we doing here?"

116

"This is our mission." He smoothed the thing in his hand, and I saw it was a piece of paper scribbled with words. "We're looking for something."

I wanted to ask him more, but he was already heading for the entrance. I gathered up the ends of my cloak and hurried after him.

We paused together at the entrance. The passage that led below lay in darkness, and a dank smell wafted from the depths. "What if there are Watchers inside?" I whispered.

Adam met my gaze. "It's still day," he said. "And they almost never go in the passages."

I had my doubts, but when he started down the crumbling steps into the blackness below, I followed.

The stone walls squeezed tighter and tighter around us the lower we went, and the light became fainter as we descended. My memories from our last visit were a blur of pale lantern light, utter blackness, and stained walls of stone. But the halls were just as dark as we left the light behind. I stopped on the stairs as the memories poured over me.

Adam paused and lit the lantern he'd brought. He waited for me, his face void of expression. I took a deep breath and nodded at him, and we moved on.

The walls were smooth stone, so smooth I could see no chisel marks. I brushed my fingers against them wonderingly. "So smooth," I breathed. I hadn't really looked at the ruins the last time we'd come. I'd been far too occupied. But now I drank in the sights of these miraculously smooth walls. The light of the lantern bounced off the floor and glimmered on the wall and ceiling, because everything was made from the same gray material. Stains colored everything brown and gray, and garbage littered the ground at our feet. My boots crunched over broken glass.

"This way." Adam turned a corner, and I followed him into a shaft of stone as tall as a well. Stairs led down in circular shape, made from the same smooth stone as the walls in the hall. Our footsteps echoed.

Words lined the walls, and I brushed my hand across them. "Engineering Corps for Human Locomotion and Oscillating Systems," I read aloud. The rest was worn away. I turned my questioning gaze to Adam. "What is that?"

"ECHLOS," he said simply.

"What?"

"Each letter stands for a word."

Understanding—and wonder—pierced me like a dart. I dropped my hand and moved on, unable to stop staring. "What do the words mean? Locomotion? Oscillating systems?"

"It's talking about the portals," Adam said. "This is where they used to study them."

My mouth fell open as that sank in. "They? You mean the ancients, the Forgotten Ones?"

He nodded.

"How did you find this out?"

A faint smile tugged at the corners of his mouth. "I'll show you."

We reached the bottom of the spiral staircase, and another corridor filled with instant, blinding light as Adam brushed his hands over a box on the wall. The glowing ceiling snapped and buzzed as if it were filled with insects. I lingered in the doorway, uncertain if it would collapse on top of me. "Is it safe? The noise..."

"Don't worry," Adam promised, brushing my arm with his hand as he started past me. "It's just the power source. We're safe."

The place where he'd touched my arm tingled faintly.

I wet my dry lips with my tongue and followed him down the corridor. My boots whispered over the grit and dust strewn over the floor, leaving smeared footprints behind me in the filth.

We reached a massive wall of stone, and I noticed the straight cracks that split the stone into square shapes just before Adam touched another box. The stone wall parted with a hiss, the pieces moving apart like a curtain, and cold, dry air rushed over us and fluttered my hair. I smelled dust and paper.

"I discovered this room a few weeks ago." Adam took a step forward, and his voice dropped to a reverent hush. "It's some kind of place of record. I think most of the documents were stored in these." He tapped an overturned gray box lying on its side. "I don't know how to get them out. But there are some papers and books, too. I've been reading and collecting them."

The gray boxes lay in disarray everywhere. Some of them had plates of glass covering their sides, and the glass was shattered and cracked. Shelves lined the walls, and I saw books, their pages scattered and torn as if they'd been thrown in a fit of rage. A few overturned tables formed a semi-circle at one side of the room, their legs extending out rigidly like animal corpses stiffened from the cold, and the light in the ceiling sputtered and flickered as if it had been somehow damaged.

"What do we do now?" My voice echoed faintly.

Adam crouched before a fallen table and began sifting through papers. "We look. I've been shuffling through these documents for weeks now, and I could use another pair of eyes."

"Are we looking for anything in particular?"

He lifted his head. I could see him mentally chewing over what to tell me. "Anything mentioning something called a PLD."

A PLD?

He didn't explain further. When our eyes met, I felt as though he were silently measuring me. I breathed in deeply, tamped down my irritation at not being told answers, and crossed the room to the shelves. I would prove myself a good addition to the operation. I would find these PLD documents.

"Don't look so dejected," Adam said after a moment, and I swear there was a hint of humor in his voice. "I don't even know what it is, and I am a seasoned Thorns operative."

"Just like you don't know what this place is?" I challenged him, but I was mostly teasing.

His snort echoed through the room. "Is that an insinuation?"

"I don't know, Adam. Did it sound like one?" I forced myself not to look at him, although I wanted to see if he smiled faintly, because I imagined he was. Instead, I grabbed a stack of books and began rifling through the pages. I didn't understand half of the words on the page.

"Officially, I don't know more than anyone else—"

"And unofficially?"

He hesitated. "I have my theories and speculations. I've been spending time here whenever I can, cataloging and mapping. I discovered this room after I received orders from my superiors, orders that told me to find information about the location of something called a PLD."

"What kind of theories?" I kept my voice even, lest my eagerness scare him off. Honestly, trying to get Adam to talk at length about *anything* was like dragging meat from the jaws of a starving dog. Especially if it had anything to do with the Thorns. But like any true-born Frost dweller, I was nothing if not stubbornly persistent.

"In Aeralis, there are great laboratories. Places of learning and science. My father worked in such a place, you see, before we fled north. I've seen things here that make me think it was once the same sort of place, only grander."

"Your father?" I knew nothing of his family except their name. "But you are Brewers."

Adam lifted his head and grinned at me. "He used to mix chemicals in a lab. It was a joke between us when we arrived. Now it's our livelihood."

I tried to imagine him living somewhere else, somewhere far south and much warmer. I couldn't picture it in my mind. "What was it like where you used to live?"

"Warm," he said. "The winters are short, and it only snows for a few months of the year. My people live in villages by the sea."

The sea? I'd heard tales of the giant bodies of water south, east, and west of us, but I'd never seen so much as a picture. "Is it like a lake?"

"Bigger," he said with a laugh. "The water stretches as far as the horizon, and waves lap the shore, and you can smell the salt in the water when the wind hits your face."

"Why would you leave something like that to come here?" I mused aloud.

He laughed, low and short. "My homeland had its own problems. The Sickness still infected some, and there was much violence. We were safer here. And I had duties with the Thorns by then."

"The Sickness," I said. I'd heard mutterings about it, a disease that plagued the southern places of the world, but I knew no details.

Adam pursed his lips. "Yes," he said, clearly not wanting to speak about it. "The extreme cold of the Frost and even Aeralis's lands kills it. It spreads best in the warmer climates."

I'd heard something to that effect before, but curiosity burned in me. I wanted to know more, but I could tell he would offer no more information. I let it drop. "You aren't Farthers, yet you said your father worked in one of their laboratories?"

"We are not Aeralians," he agreed. "But they conquered our home, and we moved to Astralux to find work. The atrocities I witnessed there convinced me to become a member of the Thorns, and the danger my family eventually found ourselves in led to our fleeing to the Frost."

"Danger?"

A muscle in his jaw tightened. He looked down at his hands and weighed his words carefully, as if he might say the wrong thing if he didn't plan first. "It's a long story."

I grimaced. I'd spoken without thinking. "I'm sorry I brought it up. I didn't mean to interrogate you."

"Don't be sorry," he said. "It's a reasonable question. Someday I'll tell you more."

Awkwardness filled the space between us in the silence that followed. I searched for a new topic, a safer one that didn't pry into his past. "These people," I said, grabbing a stack of papers and smoothing them out, "they spoke our language? How can I read these papers if they're from an ancient civilization? Should I be able to read them?"

"Why not?" Adam asked. "After all, some of the Frost dwellers are descended from the Forgotten Ones."

I dropped the papers. My mouth opened, closed, and opened again. I fumbled for words. "What did you say?"

When I turned to search his expression for any signs he was joking, I saw none.

"The Frost dwellers came from the south originally, just like your family," I said. My pulse quickened. "Our ancestors fled here to escape oppression, and the Sickness, because it was safer here, and we actually had a chance of survival. No one wants to live in the extreme cold with monsters prowling about. We're like the bluewings, hiding in the stingweed."

"I know those stories," Adam said quietly. "I've heard all the metaphors for the riddle of our existence here. But they're only a fragment of the history, a tiny piece of the picture. Some of the Frost dwellers' ancestors came from the south, yes. But a remnant of the Forgotten Ones stayed here as well, and their descendants populated the Frost villages. And part of that remnant preserved the history."

My breath left my lungs in a gasp. "How do you know this?"

"There are bits of record in these ruins," he said. "Chiseled here and there, scribbled on walls in this place. Names, accounts. I can show you. I wrote some of them down, as many as I could find. It's very old."

I almost couldn't speak, I was so astonished.

"But Adam," I said, "if the Frost dwellers are descended from the civilization that built this place, how did we ever forget about it?"

"Information is easily lost," he said. "When people have more pressing things on their minds—like survival—other things fall through the cracks with time. It's been centuries since the ancients' civilization crumbled. And the location of Echlos itself has faded into folklore. The Watchers kept people away, and time did the rest."

123

I considered this while we worked. Our people had few means of preserving history among ourselves. Maybe it had happened.

My eyes fell over a page in the bound document I'd picked up.

"Adam. Look." I held it out wordlessly. The page was covered in diagrams and scribbles. At the top, scrawled in thick ink by hand, were the letters P L D. The diagrams were indecipherable to my eyes. I squinted at them, but nothing made any sense. "Is this useful to us?"

"Bring it," he said, and I set it down to my left.

We kept searching, and after a while, my eyes started to ache from the strain of scouring faded pages while light flickered above our heads. I found no more papers inscribed with the letters PLD. Only the crumbled document with the confusing diagrams.

Finally, when I thought I couldn't stand another minute of searching, Adam stood. "We need to get back. It's getting late, and we need to stay ahead of the night."

He added the document I'd found to his sack, and we returned to the corridor. The door slid shut behind us. "It seals the room in," Adam explained. "That's why the books and papers are so well-preserved."

"How old is this place?" I wondered aloud, trailing my fingers across the smooth wall of stone.

"Hundreds of years, at least. Maybe thousands." He shouldered the bag and stepped toward the spiraling staircase. "Come on."

We retraced our steps through the corridors and up flights of steps. I stared at everything, mulling Adam's claims that my people had descended from the people who'd once built this place.

When we reached the top of the last staircase, I saw the glare of sunlight pouring through the open door ahead. Relief flickered in my chest. The scent of cold, clean air met my nose as the wind fanned our faces, and I inhaled deep lungfuls of it as we stepped out into the sunshine. "That place is a like a tomb."

"You were very brave," Adam said.

I looked at him in surprise. The wind caught his hair and blew it into his eyes, hiding them from me. I waited for him to elaborate, but he didn't. The words hung between us, and I felt surprisingly warm.

A few flakes of snow swirled around us, dragging my attention away from Adam's enigmatic statements of approval. Gray clouds lurked on the horizon, promising a storm.

"It's beginning to snow."

"Good. It'll cover our tracks."

We mounted the horses and turned them home. As they found their way back through the trees, I tried to sort out everything I'd seen and learned in the depths of the mysterious ruins.

Echlos.

Beside me, Adam rode without speaking, his hands guiding the mare effortlessly. My gelding picked his way behind the other horse. The snow had begun to fall in earnest, surrounding us in a curtain of white and enveloping the woods in a hush of quiet. I scanned the forest for signs of Watchers out of habit even though it was not yet sunset.

"What are you going to do with the things we found today?" I asked after the silence began to choke me.

At first I thought he wasn't going to answer. But then he said quietly, so quietly I almost missed it, "There's something I must decipher. I'm hoping they will help."

"Decipher?"

He shook his head, and I saw I'd get no more out of him. I let the subject drop.

Dusk had descended by the time we reached the barn. I dismounted and led the gelding into his stall. Adam unsaddled the mare.

"It's almost dark," I said. "It won't be safe to walk back." He knew that, of course, but I couldn't help saying it.

I almost missed the flash of his smile in the near-darkness. "I have my methods. But I'll need to leave this with you." He set down the pack filled with papers and books. "I'll come back for it tomorrow. Is that all right?"

"Of course," I said, reaching for it. "I'll add it to the collection of contraband."

We smiled hesitantly at each other, the terse kind of smile that comes from sharing danger and dread and all the wild elation that comes from escaping it together. And part of me felt a prickle of something else, too, but then Adam was slipping out into the gathering night and I was alone in the warm darkness of the barn with the horses nickering at my shoulder and a sack of ancient Echlos secrets at my feet. I hid the sack in the secret room and returned to the house.

~

The living area was empty when I entered it.

"Ivy? Jonn?"

The fire smoldered on the hearth, and yarn lay on the chairs. The utter stillness was palpable. I looked into my parents' old room, thinking maybe Jonn was sleeping, but the bed was empty. Upstairs was equally silent.

I returned to the main room and called their names again, and my voice splintered with panic.

126

Silence.

Dragging in a quick, frightened breath, I ran to the door. Ivy was always running off, but Jonn? Where could he be?

The yard was white, empty. The shadows of the forest were bleeding into the gathering darkness in the air. Flecks of snow swirled in front of my face. The only footprints in the yard were my own, which meant they'd left hours ago or not at all.

I returned to the house. "Jonn? Ivy?"

The barest scraping sound met my straining ears.

The bedroom.

I ran back to the doorway of my parents' room and around the bed to the very end of the room, where a wardrobe sheltered a corner from view. I stopped short at what I saw, my mouth falling open.

My brother and sister sat on the ground, surrounded by papers they were scrambling to put into one pile. They froze at my entrance. Ivy's face scrunched up in horror, and her cheeks flushed a bright red. "We did all the chores," she said quickly, as if in a last-ditch effort to distract me. "The quota's finished. Ask Jonn."

He wouldn't look at me.

"What is this?" I reached down and grabbed one of the papers before she could snatch it away. My gaze fell over it—my parents' handwriting. This was one of the documents from the secret room beneath the barn. I looked at my brother, astonishment and anger filling me in equal measures. "What are you doing?"

A muscle in his jaw flexed. He put another paper on the stack they were assembling, presumably so they could stuff it somewhere to hide it from me.

"Reading," he said. I could tell he was angry because I knew his moods better than anyone, but he was very calm as he finally looked up at me.

Ivy was not so calm, however. "We're getting involved," she said, grabbing another paper before I could get to it.

"*Involved?* With the Thorns? Absolutely not—"

"This isn't Thorns business," Jonn said.

"Those papers involve the Thorns," I growled. "Give them back."

"These are our parents' papers, and they belong to us," he said, daring me to disagree. "We're reading them. I don't think your Adam knows what's in these."

"He isn't *my* Adam," I said, and then stopped short as the rest of the words sunk in. "What's in them?"

"Nice try," he said, shaking his head. "But no. You have your duties, and I think we've found ours."

"Jonn—"

Ivy tried to yank the paper from my hands, and I lifted it out of her reach. I glared at my brother, who was now pretending to ignore me. He shuffled more papers.

"Where were you all afternoon?" she demanded. She gave up trying to get the paper in my hands and sank back to the floor.

Now it was my turn to flush. I couldn't tell them about going to Echlos. Adam would be furious. "I was busy," I hedged.

She sniffed. "You were with Adam. I saw you leaving through the window. That's when we decided to take another look at all these papers in the secret room. We found them in a box on the shelf."

"Those papers aren't supposed to be just sitting around out here. They need to stay hidden in the room beneath the barn. What if someone saw them?"

"Who's going to see them?" she muttered.

"It's dangerous!" I looked to my brother for help. He'd be against Ivy doing this, at least.

But this time, he didn't take my side. "It's our heritage."

I sucked in a breath. "The Thorns—"

"Not them," he interrupted. "I mean, it's more than that."

I stopped. Silence filled the room. "What?"

"Look," Ivy said. She fanned through the stack and pulled out a heavily creased page. "It says right here that Da's parents knew about the gate before the Thorns people ever came here."

She shoved it into my empty hand and crossed her arms over her chest. I lowered my gaze to the page. My eyes traced the words, and my heart thudded as I saw she was right. It was my father's handwriting. I recognized the scrawl. The words were too thick because of the way he had always pressed down hard on the pencil, and letters slanted hard to the right. I looked up at Jonn and found him watching me intently.

"Read it," he said.

I lowered my gaze back to the page. My mouth turned dry, and my hands clammy.

Da took me into the Frost today. He's teaching me the route to the gate along with the histories. He says this is our most treasured secret, the inheritance of the Weavers. We weave history along with yarn, he always said, and now I know it to be true. I have been sworn to secrecy. The knowledge will be mine alone to bear when I am grown, until my own children are old enough to learn it.

I breathed in deeply. My thoughts were spinning, and I struggled to corral them into a semblance of order. I met Jonn's steady gaze. "They knew about the gate before the Thorns operatives even came here?"

He shoved a hand through his hair, his angry expression slipping into one of perplexed wonder. "If Grandda was showing him these things when he reached adulthood, then it had to be so. The Thorns came into existence because of the Aerialian conflict. They've only been around for five or ten years at most. This was written before we were born."

I struggled to make sense of it all. "So the secret room below the barn wasn't built as a spy chamber for the Thorns?"

"I don't think so. But it just so happened to perfectly coincide with the Thorns agenda when they came along," he said.

I stared at them both. "So what does this all mean? Why did our family know these things?"

"I don't know," he said, "but I plan to find out."

ELEVEN

IT WASN'T ASSEMBLY day or quota day, but I went to the village the next morning anyway. I couldn't think beyond the things I'd seen at Echlos, the revelations my siblings had discovered in my parents' things, and my need to see Ann to help me sort through everything I felt. My thoughts were in a snarl, and my emotions churned thick and fast and spurred my footsteps faster and faster as I ran down the path. I was barely paying attention, so when I saw the extra soldiers filling the street and heard the creak of the Farther wagons rumbling past, my mouth went dry.

What was going on?

Fresh wagon tracks gutted the streets and turned the icy dirt to ridged mud. The soldiers yelled guttural orders at men clad in ragged clothing. Their gaunt faces and hollow eyes haunted me. As I slowed to stare, one of the soldiers turned and swept his gaze across the street. I recognized him—the brute from the quota yard who'd harassed Ann and threatened me. Tugging my cloak tighter around my face, I hurried on. I needed to find Ann. Emotional turmoil or not, I needed to know what was happening in the village. I was with the Thorns now. Such information might be critical.

The Mayor's house sat atop the highest hill in the village, and my lungs were burning by the time I reached it. I halted by the gate, gazing up as the wind fanned my cheeks and played with the edges of my cloak. The white boards of the house gleamed in the pale winter sun, and icicles glittered like fangs along the porch rails. Most of the village was made of old stone mined from the icy earth, but the Mayor's house was built from hewn boards and painted a glistening white. Delicate porches ringed the stories and extended into the gardens. It was the picture of opulence, indulgence, and exclusion.

A black coach sat in front of the house, the wheels edged in sharp spikes and the horses drawing it clad in gleaming chains.

I swallowed hard, taking note of the spikes, the chains. What was this? Had the Mayor gotten himself another symbol of his ill-purchased power, or did this belong to Officer Raine? It was clearly Aeralian, not Frost-made, and whoever drove it wanted to send the message that he was powerful, dangerous, and not to be messed with.

But I had other concerns besides locating the owner of the carriage. I needed to talk to Ann.

Instead of going to the front door, I slipped through the garden to the back and knocked on the servants' entrance. A maid poked her head out. She blinked when she saw me, and I rushed to explain. "I need to speak to

Ann Mayor. I have some yarn to show her." It was our signal. We'd arranged it months ago.

She nodded and ducked back around the door while I slipped off the porch and back into the garden. The naked branches of the trees and bushes did little to hide me, so I waited by the corner of the house. Around it, I could see the black coach.

Footsteps thudded just out of sight, and I tensed as I heard the Mayor's voice rumble in a low mutter from the porch. I pressed myself against the side of the house as figures swept down the steps toward the drive, but I caught a glimpse of them anyway.

The Mayor walked in front, flanked by two soldiers. Another man followed two paces behind. His back was to me, and all I could make out were a pair of gleaming black boots and a long black cloak with a purple stripe across the bottom. Officer Raine? But no, the walk was all wrong, and the man's hair was black instead of brown. But he walked with the same implicit authority of the Farther officer. My chest squeezed tight with apprehension.

Who was he?

The mystery figure paused before the coach, his hand on the door.

"I trust we will experience no...opposition...to our goals here?" the man in the cloak said, and the tone he used was soft and deliberate, like a caress of a knife blade against the skin.

I could see the Mayor's face from my vantage point. He nodded, his eyes flicking to the cloaked man and then to the ground. He seemed stooped, almost shrunken, as if he'd crumpled like an old parchment in the presence of this Farther.

"None," he assured the man.

"Good. I look forward to your cooperation, Mayor." He pronounced *mayor* with a sneer, as if to accentuate just how much of a joke it was.

The Mayor was silent.

The cloaked man pulled himself into the coach, the door snapped shut behind him, and one of the soldiers leaped into the driver's seat and snapped the reins. The horses broke into a jog, and the coach pulled away. I still hadn't seen the man's face, just his back, but what I'd seen told me everything I needed to know.

The Farthers must have sent their official representative from Aeralis, then—just as Ann had said they would. There would be no pretense any longer now.

We were under the heel of Aeralis' shiny black boot.

"Lia," a voice whispered at my elbow.

I jerked back from the porch and turned. Ann. "Thank goodness."

She touched my hand. "You needed to see me?"

"I...I..." My thoughts were in a tangle. I struggled to remember what I'd come to ask her. All I could see were the Farther officer's boots and the cruel spikes of the coach looking as though they'd slice anyone foolish enough to get close in half. "What's going on? There are more soldiers, wagons—and that person in the black cloak..."

"He just arrived," Ann said. "He's a nobleman from Astralux; I remember him from my visits. He came here to issue his demands to my father and have us grovel at his boots." She brushed at a curl hanging in her eyes, and I didn't miss the way her fingers trembled. "And I suppose he got his wish with the groveling. My father is about to break from the pressure." Her eyes darted to mine and then away, and her mouth tightened as she realized he would get no sympathy from me.

I looked at the ground. I was not particularly empathetic to her traitor of a father, but I was sorry she was suffering. "Do you know anything else? Who is he? What will he do?"

"He's called Korr," she said. "I don't know what he's planning—the man plans his moves like he's playing an elaborate strategy game. There'll be another Assembly tomorrow. He ordered my father to gather the village at the quota yard so he can address us. He's probably going to tell us lies about how his people sent him to help us, or some other disgusting nonsense."

Did Adam know about this? I needed to put out a signal for him tonight so I could pass on this information. "Do you think he's here to replace Raine?"

"I don't know. But they don't seem to be friends. You could have frozen milk with the look they gave each other."

I bit my lip, musing.

"Lia," Ann said, and her voice shook. "What are you going to do? You have a look in your eyes—"

"What's the Farther's name again?" I interrupted. I wouldn't let her worry about me. I couldn't. I buried her questions in my brusqueness.

"He's called Korr."

"Korr," I repeated. Even his name sounded sharp and dangerous. I shivered. I had a terrible, sinking feeling about all this.

"Don't go poking around because you're curious," she warned. "Just leave it alone. I want you to be safe."

"Safe?" I almost laughed, but the sound stuck in my throat and turned into a cough. "There is no safe. There never was, and there certainly isn't now."

She bit her lip and didn't argue with me, because there was no arguing with it. It was the truth.

~

The lantern gleamed like a fallen star against the backdrop of trees, and I watched it from my bedroom window. Ivy slept, her breathing soft and rhythmic as the sound of a running stream in thaw. Through the frosted glass of the windowpane, the woods were just a swatch of blackness against a pale night sky.

I was waiting for Adam. I'd buried the note about Korr in the snow just as he'd told me to do, but I wanted to be awake in case he knocked on the door and wanted further details.

But he didn't come, although I waited half the night with my eyes straining to see movement around the light.

I dozed at the window, and when I woke it was morning and all my muscles were stiff. For a brief moment, my mind grasped for the reason anxiety gnawed at my stomach like a rat, and then it came rushing back—Korr, on top of everything else going on. The special Assembly he'd ordered. The things they were building.

I went to the wardrobe and threw the doors open. I selected a fresh dress and bathed quickly from the basin by the bed, shivering in the cold as the water touched my skin.

I had to get into town. I had to know what was going on.

Whatever it was, it couldn't be good.

I slipped to the barn to feed the animals, and before I went in I retrieved the lantern. My heart leaped into my throat when I realized the snow had been disturbed. I dug into the heap of white—my note was gone. I raised my hand from the ice. A stone wrapped in oil cloth sat in the center of my palm, and when I unwrapped it there was a scrap of paper. A note for me. I turned it over in my hand.

I heard about the new arrival. His reputation precedes him. Do whatever you can to find out what he wants.

-A

Another note. I turned a circle in the yard, looking for tracks, but saw nothing. How had Adam retrieved it without my seeing? I'd watched half the night.

His reputation precedes him. What did that mean? Had Adam heard of this man before?

There was no time to ponder it further. I pocketed the note and went to feed the animals. I had to get to the village soon.

~

I left the house in the late morning and took the path through the Frost. The gray chill of the woods enveloped me and made me shiver just like always, but as I scanned the tree line for Watchers, my mind was skipping ahead to the prospect of Korr. Dread lay thick across my shoulders like a cloak of lead, and it weighed my steps as I reached the place where the Cage began.

The village swarmed with Farther soldiers. I looked everywhere for Ann, but all I could see was the gray of Farther uniforms and the blue cloaks of woodsmen and farmers. Villagers milled restlessly in front of the Assembly Hall, and I joined them, still watching for any sign of Ann's bright red cloak or Adam's ragged blue one. A dull sense of panic gnawed at my stomach, although I couldn't say why I felt so frightened. Korr was just another Farther. We had hundreds of them milling about now. What was the addition of one more to the mix?

The crunch of wheels against street sludge signaled the approach of the carriage, and everyone drew back as the black Aeralian coach I'd seen yesterday drew up before the Hall. The door snapped open, and those gleaming boots descended, followed by the man himself.

My throat closed up, smothering my gasp as I saw Korr's face.

It was Gabe.

TWELVE

MY THOUGHTS SHATTERED. I was momentarily incapable of movement.

Gabe?

No. It couldn't be. It was impossible. I gulped in a breath as shock numbed my blood and chilled my skin. He'd gone through the gate. He'd left us forever, it couldn't be—

The Farther stepped from the shadow of the coach into the sunlight, and I exhaled sharply as I realized the truth.

Not Gabe.

But someone so like Gabe that I'd been fooled. His face, his eyes, his movements... he was almost identical to the Farther fugitive who I'd hidden in my barn months ago.

There were some differences, age being the most obvious. Korr, although still a young man, looked several years older than Gabe. His eyes and hair were darker, and his nose was perfectly straight, unlike Gabe's crooked, broken one. Sophistication, control, and an air of cruelty clung to him like a second cloak.

Otherwise, however, they could be twins.

What did it mean? My mind refused to put the pieces together to understand it even as the truth lurked like a shadow at the very edges of my consciousness. Every thought in my mind had frozen. The information I'd absorbed had crystallized and splintered into something hard and painful.

Korr stepped forward, flanked by two Farther soldiers. His eyes swept the crowd as if he was searching for something, and his gaze lingered on each face as if he was memorizing our features. The villagers stood as motionless as trees while he moved through the crowd, inspecting us all. I wanted to shrink away into nothingness, but I didn't dare move. Fleeing or turning away would attract the most attention. And even if I'd had the courage, or the reason, I didn't think my feet would have unglued themselves from the ground. I was in too much shock.

When his gaze reached me, every muscle in my body grew tight, and the silence rang in my ears as loud as a scream. Korr's gaze lingered on me for an impossible span of time—was it five seconds or five minutes? Sweat broke out across my palms and upper lip and dripped between my shoulder blades. My skin tingled as the perspiration met the freezing air. I was a prisoner of those eyes.

Finally, he broke eye contact and moved on. I sucked in air and tried not to tremble visibly. My legs felt like jelly, and my stomach was sick from clenching so hard.

A cruel apparition of my former love had just stared me in the eyes with an expression that promised terrible things. A violent shudder shook me, and I clamped my lips together to keep from making any noise. I hadn't been prepared for this nightmare.

A hand brushed my wrist, and I slowly turned my head.

Adam.

His dark eyes cut into me, reading the turmoil on my face, and he moved closer as if trying to get a better look at Korr. But his long fingers slipped into mine and squeezed once, as if he was giving me the strength to keep standing. My stomach tightened, warmth spilled through me, and I found I could breathe again as we stood with our fingers touching through our gloves and our eyes watching Korr move toward the front of the Assembly Hall. And no one saw us—every eye in the crowd was fixed on Korr.

Wait. What was I doing, holding Adam's hand?

I pulled my fingers away ever so gently. Adam's expression didn't change, but the space between his eyebrows wrinkled slightly. Was he angry? I looked, but he was watching Korr, and I could see the dawning realization that crossed his face as he made the connection that the nobleman could almost be Gabe's twin.

Korr ascended the steps of the Assembly Hall. When he reached the top, he turned on his heel and gazed over the crowd, a smile playing over his mouth in a way that looked exactly like a crueler, more sadistic Gabe. His black cloak fluttered in a gust of wind, and his long dark hair blew into his eyes and around his mouth. He lifted one gloved hand and flicked the strands away, and shivers ran over my skin like a thousand tiny spiders. The move was so casual and yet so deliberate. It spoke volumes about the man.

A movement to the left caught my eye, and I spotted Officer Raine and his men shoving through the crowd at the far corner of the Assembly Hall. Raine's mouth was set in a scowl, and his hand rested on the pistol at his waist as he strode forward, his shoulders jerked with every stride he took. I wondered if he'd even been informed about this gathering. Had Korr and the Mayor made arrangements behind his back?

The company of Farther soldiers following Raine reached the steps and halted. Raine crossed his arms and regarded Korr as if issuing a silent challenge.

Suddenly, danger hung over the scene like the too-bright feel of the air after a flash of lightning.

But Korr only smiled.

"People of the Frost," he said, speaking loudly enough that his voice filled the square. "I can see by your faces that you are apprehensive about me. And I don't blame you." He spoke conversationally, as if we were all confidants chatting together over a meal.

The people around me shifted, and a few murmured dissent. I exchanged glances with Adam.

What game was the nobleman playing?

Korr raised one gloved hand as if to quiet the mutters. "Oh, I know the marks against me. I am an

Aeralian. I am one of the oppressors. I am of noble, Farther blood." He ticked off his points on one hand, still smiling. "But let me assure you—I am here to help." He glanced at Raine and grinned wider, as if he knew a delicious secret nobody else did. "Our people have not exactly been endearing ourselves to you, have they? Take Officer Raine. I know the man well, and I'll wager he's not lauded around your fireplaces at night."

A quiet storm of whispers filled the air. Raine appeared to be holding himself still by sheer willpower. The soldiers behind him exchanged glances. I frowned. There was some sort of history between them. I could sense it. Korr was baiting him...but why?

"You might secretly think in your hearts that he's harsh. Well, he's a soldier," Korr drawled, shooting Officer Raine a smile that pretended to be indulgent. His eyes were razor-sharp and full of malice. "He's not prone to coddling. Believe me, he has his own reputation back home. Have you ever heard how he acquired his limp?"

Officer Raine's lips whitened with rage.

We were all in the palm of his hand now. No one moved or spoke. The mention of such a story promised incredible things. Enemy or not, Korr had intrigued us.

Korr tipped his head to one side, as if considering the value of recounting it. The moment stretched out, every second tingling with tension.

"Ah," he said finally. "Some other time, although I assure you, the story is quite a heroic one."

Raine's face was turning a mottled purple.

"But enough about such unpleasant topics," Korr said. "Let's talk about me." He paused, surveying us, smiling again. "I've been sent to act as consul on behalf of the Aeralian government. That means I've been sent to represent you, good people. I'm sure you're well aware of our situation in Aeralis. Our nation is at war. We need all the friends we can find. And if soldiers can't quite romance the people of the Frost and keep the monsters away at night, well…" He dimpled. "Our mighty Emperor decided to give a nobleman a try."

Murmurs began to hiss around me again, louder this time, but I couldn't catch anyone's whispered words. My own mind was spinning. Nobleman. From Gabe's family. Sent by the Emperor? It was just all too convenient. What was he *really* doing here?

"We'll have to get to know one another better, I think," Korr continued. "And as your consul, I will make myself available to anyone who wishes to speak with me. I want to know all your concerns, your observations, your needs. And I will be keeping a close eye on every one of you."

It was not so much a promise as a threat. Was he here to spy?

"I think we're going to get along well," Korr finished. He shot a look at Officer Raine, whose hands had knotted into fists. "Did you want to say a few words, Officer?"

Raine didn't take the bait. He swallowed his fury and declined stiffly, and then the Mayor shuffled up the steps and took Korr's place as meekly as a child.

"Quota will be increased by half," he announced, "to accommodate the workers building the consulate."

Everyone around me inhaled sharply. I felt as though the air had been sucked from my lungs. They were increasing our quota by half? How would we find the time? We were worked to the bone as it was.

"That is all," the Mayor said sharply.

We were dismissed.

The crowd parted numbly as I locked gazes with Adam. I wanted to ask him questions, but he gave me an infinitesimal shake of his head. Not here.

We parted ways without speaking. I knew he'd find me later, perhaps even come by the farm tonight. And I needed to find Ann.

I searched the streets for her, but saw no sign of her bright red hood. I passed the quota yard, and beyond it I spotted the walls of the consulate Korr had mentioned. Already, the building gleamed coldly in the sunlight, an alien thing in the midst of our wooden houses. It was going up quickly, much more quickly than I could understand. I wondered with a stab of foreboding what the Watchers would think of this development. Would the extra Farther technology drive them further into a rage?

Finally I gave up on finding Ann. I needed to get home. Jonn and Ivy would be worried sick.

Just as I turned the corner to head for the Cage, a hand grabbed my upper arm. I whirled.

Ann.

"Oh," I breathed, grabbing her tight. "I was worried—"

She was extra pale today, and her cloak seemed to envelop her slender frame even more than usual. More dark circles ringed her eyes, and the cut on her cheek had scabbed over. "Don't worry," she murmured, her eyes darting around as she spoke. "I'm the Mayor's daughter, remember? They can't touch me." But her expression belied her words—she grimaced as she spoke. I noticed her hands looked thinner, more fragile than normal, and her lips were almost colorless.

I took in her appearance. "Are you sure you're all right?"

"I'm fine," she interrupted. "It's just all these Watcher attacks..." She averted her eyes as a pair of Farther soldiers passed us. "And...I wanted to ask you something. A favor."

"Anything," I said without hesitation.

"The Elder families are gathering for a private party with Officer Raine and Korr. It's all Raine's idea, you see...a ploy to prove he is in control here, and we all get along. I will host the gathering at my father's house." She hesitated, biting her lip. "We are short a few servants, and I thought—"

My heart turned over as the words sank in. Servants. Shame rushed over me. She wanted me to work in her home as a servant. "Oh."

Her face pinched. "We're paying people in food. It will be like quota. And I know you need extra, so I thought..."

In my head, I saw the note again. *Do whatever you can to find out what he wants.*

If I did this, I'd be able to keep an eye on Korr. Wasn't that what Adam wanted?

"All right," I said, closing my eyes and gritting my teeth together. It was the most abhorrent idea I'd ever had, but it was an opportunity and I wasn't going to waste it.

"Yes?" She took a deep breath and let it out. Clearly she'd expected me to refuse. Her relief was palpable. "Thank you, Lia. You're a true friend."

Or a true idiot, I thought darkly.

Silence washed between us.

"I've seen Everiss," she said, changing the subject with a note of desperation in her voice, and the way she said it made my stomach twist, because her tone made it sound as if she was warning me to prepare myself. What else could have possibly happened to that family?

"How is she?"

"She..." Ann trailed off and made a useless gesture with one hand. "Well, she's been avoiding me. But things have been hard for her family."

"Why would she be avoiding you?"

"I don't know. I've seen her keeping company with someone and it makes me wonder, though."

"Did she reconcile with her fiancé?"

"No...the blacksmith's son. Leon, I think he's called."

Understanding pierced me like a knife. I gaped at her as the pieces fell into place. Everiss was avoiding Ann, and hanging out with Leon...

No. It couldn't be. Everiss and Ann had been close friends since they were babies.

But the certainty gnawed at me, and I felt sick. "Are you absolutely certain she's avoiding you?"

Ann clasped her arms across her chest and turned her face against the wind. "I'm not the most beloved person right now, Lia, thanks to my connections to the Farthers."

"Thanks to your *father's* connections," I muttered. I looked at the scab on her cheek and my blood simmered. "I don't understand this madness. Turning on friends, changing loyalties..."

"People have to do what they can to live." She tucked a strand of hair behind her ear and tried to smile, but it didn't reach her eyes.

I squinted at the sun instead of replying. Everiss's betrayal was too upsetting. I couldn't pretend to understand it. "I need to get back."

"Wait," she said quickly. "I need to speak with you about something."

I paused, waiting for her to explain. She shook her head. "Not here. Tomorrow, in the garden behind my house? Please."

"Of course," I said, but anger was still seething in my veins.

We embraced, and then I headed for the gate, and home.

~

Thoughts swirled thick and fast as snowflakes in my mind as I worked on quota that night. My ruminations jumped between Everiss, Ann, Raine, and Korr...but mostly I thought about Korr. He looked too much like Gabe. They were both from noble families. It was not a coincidence—they must be related. Cousins? Brothers, even? But this man was cruel, calculating, and clearly working with the Aeralian dictator.

What was going on?

Gabe clearly had left out some important details about his life when he'd told me things. This thought clung in my mind like a cobweb, sticking all my other thoughts together, refusing to let me go.

"How can you work as a servant for the Farthers?" Ivy demanded, pacing from the window to my side and breaking into my thoughts. In his chair by the fire, Jonn sat silent and grim. He didn't look at me as he worked at the yarn. We still weren't on good terms since our fight.

"It's for Ann," I said wearily. I was tired of explaining, and I had not yet told them about the resemblance between Gabe and Korr. The words stuck to my tongue when I tried to speak them. I felt bone-weary and sick. Tossing the yarn down, I went to the window and peered out.

"You're expecting Adam Brewer?" Jonn asked from his chair. His voice was low, flat.

"I..." I had been hoping he'd come. I hadn't put out the lantern, but we had things we needed to discuss.

As if on cue, a faint knock sounded at the door.

We all flinched; Jonn and Ivy looked at me. I drew in a deep breath and crossed the room. I paused, my hand hovering over the handle.

A Watcher wouldn't knock, and a Farther knew better than to wander around at night.

I lifted the bar and pulled it open.

Adam's dark eyes met mine. He leaned against the frame, his cloak fluttering in the cold wind that swept around him and into the house. Behind him, the snowy yard gleamed silver in the darkness, and I saw the outline of his footprints. Something else crisscrossed the snow, too.

"Watcher tracks?" I whispered.

He nodded with a jerk of his head. That was when I noticed the blood blooming on his sleeve.

"Adam?"

I grabbed his shirt and tugged him inside, slamming the door shut behind me. The chill from the outside air lingered around us as I pulled away the fabric. It was sliced to ribbons and stained a blackish red.

"Was it Watchers?" Ivy ran to my side, her voice squeaking. I felt Jonn's attention sharpen, and he pushed himself up to see, but he didn't speak.

Adam met my eyes, and his gaze was full of tiredness and reluctance and something else I couldn't name, something that tugged at me deep inside. It was as if he were asking me to fix something that had been broken, but not his arm.

"Watchers," he confirmed, the word almost a sigh.

I helped him to the fire and then hurried into the kitchen for the kettle and a bottle of whiskey. When I returned, he'd already rolled back the torn sleeve of his shirt. Ivy hovered around him, and Jonn had pushed himself up to see. I put the kettle on the boil in case we needed hot water, then sank by Adam's side and reached for his arm.

The cut was a clean one, almost as if it had been made by a knife. Among the wild things of the Frost, only Watcher claws were so sharp. Rivulets of red beaded along the sliced skin and traced a scarlet path down his forearm.

Adam winced but didn't make a sound as I dabbed it with whiskey from the kitchen and then bound it with strips of clean rags. He was pale but resolute, and he looked at Jonn as if he were issuing—or accepting—a challenge.

"Are you going to tell us what happened?" I asked after I'd finished.

"A Watcher came out of nowhere. I didn't see it. I felt the wind rush over my head and heard the growl, and I ran. But the creature caught my arm with its claws."

"Another attack," I murmured.

"It's the presence of the Farthers, isn't it?" Jonn leaned forward in his chair. "It's stirring them up. They can sense all the foreignness of the materials, the technology they've brought into the village. They're getting restless."

Adam raised his eyebrows in silent agreement. "I think so, yes."

"You knew this," Jonn continued, his tone turning accusatory. "You knew how the dangers were increasing, and yet you've dragged my sister into this mess anyway."

I turned astonished eyes on him. "Jonn!"

There was a brief, shivering silence. Adam's eyes narrowed slightly. "I did not drag her into anything," he said. "She made the choice herself. But we need her. And yes, it is dangerous. I won't deny it."

"Our parents *died*, Brewer."

"Many have died," Adam said icily. "And Frost dwellers aren't squeamish about danger. But this isn't about that, is it? It's about something else."

"How dare you—"

"Stop," I interrupted. "We're all in danger, and if I don't do something about the Farthers then it will only get worse. I'm doing this for you, Jonn, and you, Ivy."

"If we're all in danger, then why won't you let me help?" Jonn shouted.

Well. There was the crux of the matter. I was shocked out of a reply at his outburst, so I just looked at him.

"Leave your sister alone," Adam said. "This is between you and her, and it isn't about the Thorns."

"This doesn't involve you," Jonn said.

"Both of you," I snapped. "Stop it."

They glared at each other. My brother's breath came in gasps. His gaze slid to my face and then away, and a stain of bright color leaked across his cheekbones. The fire sparked and crackled. Adam glared at the wall, his arms crossed tightly. Ivy made a soft sound that was something between a whimper and a sob, breaking the thick silence.

"Stop," I said again. "We're upsetting Ivy."

"I'm not a child," she grumbled.

Jonn and Adam glared at each other like two wolves defending their respective territories, but they didn't say anything else.

My eyes fluttered closed with short-lived relief as the pit of my stomach churned with unease. I felt like a bird caught in a net that was ever-so-slowly tightening. So many opposing loyalties. So many opposing considerations.

When I opened them, Adam was watching me.

I still needed to speak to him about Korr. But how would I find the opportunity with my siblings hovering around?

A plan formed in my head.

"Listen," I said. "I think you should stay, just like last time. You can make a bed here by the fire."

"I'll be fine—"

I touched his shoulder. "Your arm is injured, it's very cold, and the Watchers are still out there. Stay, Adam. Don't be foolish."

He looked at my hand on his arm and then at my face, and I couldn't interpret his expression. "All right," he said slowly.

"All right," I repeated, withdrawing my hand. "Good. We'll make you a bed by the fire just like before."

I gathered up the yarn and put it away while Ivy climbed the steps to our room. Jonn fumbled with his crutches.

"I'll get the blankets for Adam," Ivy said.

Adam shoved his hands in his pockets. He filled the room with his presence, and the scent of pine and snow permeated the air. My gaze kept straying to him as I cleared up our quota and packed it in a basket. Jonn caught me looking, and his brow furrowed. I bit my lip and turned away as my cheeks reddened.

My sister returned with her arms full of blankets. "I need more quilts," she announced.

"There's some in Ma and Da's room," Jonn said, and threw me a meaningful look.

He hobbled for the door, and I followed. I shut the door behind me and leaned against it, watching as he limped to the bed.

"Jonn..."

"I'm sorry," he said, without turning around. "I shouldn't have gotten so angry. I'm just...scared."

"I know."

He slumped back on the bed and stared hard at the ceiling. "I can't do anything. I can't help you, protect you, nothing. I'm useless."

My voice cracked. "You're not useless—"

"You'd better get him these blankets." He tugged at one of his quilts, pushing it toward me. My mother's

Frost quilt, all shades of white and silver with a ribbon of black cutting through it.

I grabbed the blanket and bunched it in my arms, searching for the right words to say to him as I hugged the quilt close and inhaled its scent. "You understand why I'm doing it, don't you? Why I'm working with the Thorns?"

His throat bobbed as he swallowed. "I understand," he said finally, and his voice rasped with emotion. "I just wish..."

He left the last bit unspoken. We both knew what he wished. No reason to say it out loud.

"I'd better get this to Adam." I patted the quilt, suddenly eager to be out of the room as awkwardness filled it.

Jonn frowned. "Are you sure about what you're doing there?"

"What do you mean?" I squeaked, avoiding his eyes.

He just shrugged.

I closed the door behind me and leaned against it, gathering my thoughts and emotion up and stuffing them deep inside me. I took a deep breath and returned to the main room.

Adam crouched by the fire, fussing with the blankets Ivy had brought him. The firelight flickered over his shoulders and face and illuminated his hands. When I entered, he sat back on his heels and waited.

I offered him the quilt. He accepted it silently, and our hands brushed. A tingle slipped up my arm, a spark, and I drew my hand back quickly. He looked up and held

157

me in place with his gaze, and suddenly the air was thick as glue, and I was stuck in it.

A nervous sensation fluttered in my stomach. Unspoken words clouded the air. I remembered the way he'd taken my hand in the village, and how it had comforted me.

Are you sure about what you're doing there? my brother had asked.

I blanched. I wasn't sure.

Was it wrong for me to feel something for him, when I had also felt something for Gabe? My heart still ached for the Farther boy I'd known for only a few short weeks, but...he was gone. Forever.

I didn't know what to think.

Adam was watching me, his eyes opaque. What did he see when he looked at me? An asset, a necessary connection, a duty to my dead parents? Or something else?

The silence had stretched too long. I was staring. I blinked and licked my lips, finding a place on the floor to look at instead. "I'm sorry about what my brother said."

Adam settled back against my brother's chair and crossed his arms over his knees. He leaned his head back and shut his eyes. "He's not angry at you or me. He's angry at himself."

"How do you know?"

He opened one eye. "You don't get to where I am without knowing how to read people."

The words slid off my tongue, unbidden. "And what do you read in me?"

He lifted his head and looked at me without answering right away. His gaze was a caress, and my stomach twisted. Had he always looked at me this way? Or had it begun over the last few weeks, when we'd spent so much time together?

"You love your siblings deeply."

Was that all? "I don't think you need any insight to guess that."

"You think you have to protect them, shield them," he continued quietly, ignoring my retort. "But you're wrong. They're strong, just like you. They grew up in the same perilous place. They have what it takes."

My cheeks flushed. "I can't be sure, and I'm not willing to be wrong."

He frowned. "Holding them back will only hurt them, and you."

"If you'd lost loved ones the way I have, you would feel the same."

"I have lost loved ones," he said quietly.

I bit my lip, and the stillness wrapped around us again. I waited for him to say more, but he didn't. The moment had shattered, and the warmth that had been drawing us closer bled away, leaving coldness in its wake.

I paced to the window and peaked through the shutters, more because I wanted to avoid looking at him than for any fear of finding monsters outside. My breath fogged the glass. "Ann asked me to help serve at a gathering for Officer Raine and the new Farther."

"Really?" He leaned forward with interest. "You said yes, I assume."

"Of course." I studied the yard. Everything was still, silent. "What do you think about Korr?" I left my implications unspoken, but they leaked into my voice.

He turned his head toward the fire. "Obviously your Gabe left a few things out of his story, didn't he?"

My Gabe. It was like a slap.

"Don't do that," I said.

"No?" Adam ran fingers through his hair and ground his teeth together, the only sign that he might be as nervous and conflicted as I was. He turned his head toward the fire.

We were dancing around the topic like moths around a flame, teasing and testing but never landing. I turned back to the window and leaned my forehead against the glass.

He wasn't *my Gabe*, and I was beginning to think he never was. I'd known so little about him, and although we'd had an intense connection, had it been based on more fantasy than truth? Of course, Gabe had never had any obligation to tell me everything about him. But I'd believed he'd shared his situation with me, and now I questioned that. Had I been completely mistaken about him?

The thought made my stomach churn.

"Korr," he said, pulling me out of my thoughts and back to the conversation at hand. "Obviously he has some other agenda."

I took a breath and let him steer the conversation back to something safe. "He's Aeralian, and a noble. Related to...well." I didn't say Gabe's name, but we both knew. "Obviously they have some family connection."

"If he's looking for the Farther, he's more than two months too late, and he doesn't seem like the kind of person who makes those kinds of mistakes."

I nodded. He'd been so deliberate at the Assembly Hall, as if he knew the effect every word he spoke would have on both Officer Raine and the crowd.

"He was toying with Raine," Adam continued thoughtfully. "They must have some sort of history. There's tension between them. Dueling political aspirations, maybe?"

I snorted. "Seems more like a personal vendetta to me. Korr is making Raine look like a fool and he's enjoying every second of it, too. And I doubt the officer can do anything about it, seeing as Korr's a noble." I remembered the way Raine had put his hand on his pistol, as if he wanted nothing more than to yank it out and shoot it. But he'd remained silent and still.

Adam leaned his head back and laced both arms behind his neck. His eyes gleamed in the firelight. "True," he agreed.

"So what could he want?"

He sighed. "I want you to do everything you can to find out more at that gathering of the Elders you've been so fortunate as to obtain an invite to."

"An invite?" I snorted. "I'll be slaving in the kitchens, Adam. She asked me, so perhaps she wants me close for comfort, but I don't even merit an actual invitation. It's an insult."

"It's an opportunity," he said. "I'll make sure to be in town that night, as close to the Mayor's house as I can get, so we might be able to communicate, and I'll be searching for information too. But you have a unique source of information that I do not, and a way to obtain access."

A unique source of information. He meant Ann. It was not an inaccurate way of describing her, but it was rather cold. Was that all we were to him? Sources of information, sources of assistance? Was that all *I* was to him?

His face revealed nothing. His expression was neutral, unreadable.

"After," he said, "I'll come by the farmhouse, and we can discuss what we learned."

I watched the firelight play over his face. "How do you dare to travel the Frost at night, knowing the Watchers have become even more restless?"

A frown tugged at his lips. "I have my secrets, just like everyone else," he said. "Maybe sometime I'll show you."

Something else lingered beneath the surface of the statement, something heavy and hesitant and full of promise. I paused, wanting to accept it but afraid. The moment stretched, thickened. His eyes flicked over my face, and he leaned away and rubbed a hand over his eyes.

"Goodnight, Lia Weaver."

"Goodnight, Adam."

I crept up the stairs and slipped into bed beside Ivy, my mind spinning with weariness and questions.

THIRTEEN

THE TREES STOOD out starkly against the bird's wing-blue sky as I traveled the path to the village. As I walked, I turned the events of the previous night over in my mind. Adam. Me. Gabe.

It was snarled up like a tangle of yarn in my mind. I cared about Gabe deeply, but he was gone. And there were things he hadn't told me about himself, important things.

Did that matter?

I reached the Cage and slipped inside, shivering as the shadows striped my skin and the Farthers' gazes searched me. I reached the entrance to the village and hurried through the streets. The wind-scrubbed stone walls and buildings formed a tunnel of gray and I wandered through it in a fog of thought.

Someone called my name, and I turned, my heart beating fast. Blackcoats?

But it was Jullia, her stained hands gesturing at me from the alleyway.

"How are you?" I asked. Once, the Dyers had been among the most well-dressed of the village. Now, Jullia's hair fell in wispy strands around her face, and threads hung from the edges of her dress. Her pale cloak, previously soft and white as milk, had turned dishwater gray.

"We manage," she said briskly, but then her mouth softened and gave me a smile like it was a peace offering. "I wanted to thank you for before, for helping us. My sister has been...busy..." she trailed off.

My response stuck in my throat. I remembered what Ann had told me. Everiss was working with the Blackcoats now.

Jullia blinked. She scrutinized my face, and then she frowned. "You know, don't you?"

I fumbled for words. "Know what?" I managed, and then cringed at such a banal and obvious response.

"About Everiss's new...alliance?" A line formed between her eyebrows, and she fidgeted with the edge of her sleeve. "You and Ann helped us the other day, and I just wanted to say..." She breathed in and out quickly. "Regardless of what my sister chooses to do, I am grateful for your help. And—and in the future, I'd be happy to help you with anything you need, too."

A lump filled my throat. I nodded, unable to find an appropriate verbal reply. She looked at me a moment longer, shifted her weight from foot to foot, then wrapped her cloak tight around her shoulders and headed back the way she'd come.

I was left standing in the street, feeling curiously sad and whole at the same time.

The stamp of footsteps jerked me back to reality as a pair of soldiers passed me, their gazes sharp. I ducked my head and pressed on for Ann's house. I would speak with her and then head home again. I had a great deal of work to do now that quota had been increased.

Ann was waiting for me in the gardens behind her house. She stood in the snow, beneath one of the ornamental red pines that ringed the glass greenhouse and shielded the garden from the rest of the village. Standing there all alone, she looked thin and cold and impossibly fragile, like a baby bird fallen from its nest.

She lifted her head as I approached. "You came."

She sounded...disappointed?

"You asked me to," I said, and a chuckle bubbled up in my throat.

But the laughter died on my lips when a man in a black cloak stepped out from behind the pines. Shock flashed over my skin like cold water. I couldn't move, couldn't breathe.

Korr.

"Lia Weaver," he drawled, pinning me in place with his bright, cold eyes and precise smile. "I remember you. You were at the gathering a few days ago, looking incensed at my speech." His tone was perfectly composed, polite, as if we were discussing the weather. But there was an edge of danger underneath. He had a proverbial blade to my throat, and we both knew it.

Shivers started at my knees and worked up my body. My hands and lips felt numb. My feet wouldn't move. My mouth wouldn't work. My thoughts turned in frightened circles. Did he know about Gabe? Did he know I was with the Thorns? What was he going to do?

"Surprised I remembered you? I have a knack for faces, they say. I never forget one once I've seen it." He dimpled and tapped his cheek with one long, gloved finger. "And I must say yours looks rather familiar to me, although I've never met you before. I wonder why."

I was numb, white, blank as snow. I couldn't breathe, couldn't make sense of anything that was happening. I saw everything as if I were a casual observer looking out a window: Ann, her curls shining in the pale sunlight; Korr, his dark hair blowing in the wind and his teeth gleaming behind his smirk as he tapped a gloved finger against his lips; and me, my ragged little cloak curling around my body as if to hide me from the nightmare unfolding around me. I stared at him as he stepped closer, stopping beside Ann. A memory floated to the forefront of my mind: Adam saying a word softly, hesitantly. *Torture.*

Did he know what I was?

"Your friend has been most obliging by luring you here," Korr continued, his gaze playing over my face. "I've heard your name a few times among the soldiers...apparently you recently had a little incident in the quota yard?"

My blood was ice. My lungs were wood. Should I speak, or remain silent? I looked at Ann for help, but she was studying the snow at her feet as if frozen water were the most fascinating thing she'd ever laid eyes on.

"You're quite the silent one. Well, I thought we could become better acquainted. I hope you don't mind?" He waved a hand, and I saw his coach waiting just beyond the house.

My heart sunk like a stone. I couldn't run. There was nowhere to go. I was trapped.

Ann still wouldn't look at me.

She'd lured me here. She'd known…

Finally, I found my voice. I stared hard at my friend. "What have you done?"

"Lia, it isn't…it isn't what it seems." Ann held the edges of her cloak with both fists, her knuckles the grayish-white color of dirty snow.

"Yes, don't blame your friend," Korr said in a pleasant tone. "I left her little choice but cooperation, and she's been very helpful."

Ann bit her lip so hard a seam of blood appeared beneath her teeth.

"Ann," I whispered. "Why?"

The wind blew between us, and she didn't reply.

"This is all so deliciously melodramatic," Korr drawled. "But I'm pressed for time. And I want to get this over quickly. Shall we go?"

Get this over quickly.

This.

Me.

I wanted to retch my breakfast in the snow.

He extended his hand, a mockery of an invitation, and I stepped toward the coach. He followed, keeping close enough that I knew I was completely under his control. There would be no escape.

I twisted my head to look back at my friend, the one I loved and trusted. She stood motionless, her arms dangling, her bloodied lips pressed together tightly and a single tear running down her cheek.

~

Korr sat with his head leaned against the plush back of the coach seat, his eyes narrowed into slits as he gazed out the window. He ran his hand up and down the glass, a restless gesture that unnerved me. I huddled in the opposite corner, a miserable loop of scenarios playing through my mind. Would they torture the truth out of me? Would they take Jonn and Ivy, confiscate the farm? What would Adam do? How would he find out?

Did I dare try to run?

The coach stopped before the consulate building. The prefabricated structure looked utterly alien, the gleaming metal walls rising up from the wooden buildings around it, the whole thing ugly as a scar against the ancient stone architecture of the village.

I climbed out of the coach, my hands shaking. My boots crunched on the icy dirt that surrounded the building site as I crossed the yard, and Korr followed, laying one gloved hand on my shoulder and pushing me forward. Soldiers blocked the gate, and any thought of running died at the press of his hand on my shoulder.

The sound of workers' hammers clanged and clattered around us as he escorted me to the door and ushered me inside.

The interior offered little to see. Bands of light gleamed in golden stripes across the floor of a dark hallway. The hammering was muted now, and it echoed faintly, as if we were deep underground. Far away, I heard the metallic whine of grinding gears, and the clang of heavy steel slamming down. I jerked. Sweat formed on my palms and dripped down my back.

"This way," he said, pushing me toward a door at the end of the hall.

What was he going to do to me?

The door opened into a small room with a single desk and a chair. Light streamed from a window set high in the wall and pooled against the far wall.

Korr paced around the desk, half of his face catching in the beam. The reddish brilliance lit his eyelashes and the ends of his hair and threw shadows across his mouth and eyes.

He looked cruel, almost animalistic.

"Now," he said, leaning over the desk and boring his gaze into mine. "Let's talk."

I licked my dry lips and tried to think of what to do, what to say, but Adam's words about torture were the only thought that kept surfacing in my swirl of mental panic. Fresh sweat blossomed across my shoulder blades. A pang of terror stabbed my chest, and I clamped my lips shut in desperation. The secrets I carried were like a dead corpse across my shoulders, weighing me down, and Korr's eyes watched me with nimble observance. I dared not move or speak for fear of betraying myself somehow.

I looked away from his face, at the wall behind him. I realized he'd pinned up a map of the Frost, a much nicer one than any I'd ever seen. Our village sat in the center, and the paths through the Frost shot out from it like spokes on a wheel. There was the river that separated us from the Farthers, tracing the edge of the map, a thin thread of blackish blue. There was the mountains, the lake of ice, the roads to the other villages, Riverhaven and Brackworth and others so far away that we rarely heard anything from them. A thought flew through my head—had they been taken over just as we had?—but Korr shifted, and the movement snatched my attention back to the present.

"Weaver," he mused. "Your family makes the yarn and the thread. Do you make the village clothes, too? Or is that the Tailor's job?"

A vein throbbed just below my jaw. Was he making *small talk* before he tortured me?

"Come, come," Korr drawled. "Don't be so shy. I know a great deal about you already, Lia Weaver. Your parents were killed by the monsters that roam the night, and now you care for your crippled brother and impetuous young sister alone." He paused, waiting. When I didn't make a sound, he straightened and flashed me a cold smile. "Don't be so afraid, girl. Answer my questions, and I will make it worth your while."

"What questions?" My voice sounded rusty to my ears. It was too loud, too desperate.

"The girl speaks." He smirked.

I clamped my lips shut again.

171

Korr slid one finger over the edge of his desk, brushing away a line of dust. "How well do you know the Frost?"

"I live in the midst of it," I said simply.

"That must be hard. All alone out in the wilderness, so far from the others, unprotected from the wild things of the woods." He paused, deliberate and quiet. "Why do you live so far from the rest of the village?"

Fear spiked in my chest. I thought of the papers in the room beneath the barn, my father's journals about his father and the histories. Was there some other reason that we lived so far from the others? And why was Korr asking me?

"It is our home." I spoke before I could stop myself. "It was my parents' home. We will stay in our home despite the danger, because it is ours."

He tipped his head to one side, studying me. "You Frost dwellers are a stubborn lot."

I didn't reply to that.

"Two months ago, a fugitive escaped our Aeralian borders and crossed into your lands."

My heart skipped a beat. Gabe, then. I dared not say anything to betray my knowledge that he was related to the fugitive. I stayed silent. I forced the muscles in my face to stay slack, expressionless.

Korr rounded the desk. He stopped in front of me, and we stood toe to toe. "The fugitive escaped. He was not recaptured."

"What are you asking?" I said. I made my voice as even as possible.

"I am looking for a place of legend," Korr said. His voice lowered, dropping to a purr. " In the past, some have called it Ech, Echo, the Place of Echoes, the Ancient City. It's true name is Echlos."

I forced myself to be still, to be nonreactive. My eyes didn't widen. My mouth didn't fall open. But my hands prickled with fresh perspiration.

Echlos.

The word felt wrong coming from his mouth, like a secret I never imagined I'd hear uttered aloud. My skin turned to ice and I held very still lest I shatter. Lest I slip up and give something away in my expression. My pulse pounded in my throat and wrists and roared in my ears.

He bent over me, and his dark gaze bored into mine. "You live on the fringes of the wild. If anyone might catch a glimpse of this place, it would be someone like you."

He spoke softly, precisely, and each syllable was a promise of something malevolent. But he was smiling, as if we were having a friendly conversation. His eyes challenged me. "You're in a prime spot to gather information."

I was trembling all over. My legs were jelly, my stomach a tight knot.

"I heard about your little stunt the other day," he said. "With the soldier? A dangerous move for a Frost dweller to make, don't you think?"

I licked my lips. They had become very dry.

"Officer Raine is threatening death for anyone found working against him, but I have clout that he does not. I could protect anyone who came to me first."

My heart thudded.

"You're in a precarious place, Lia Weaver. But if you bring me information, I can help you. I can make sure Raine doesn't notice you. I can make sure your little farm and little family stay protected. You'd be well rewarded."

All I could see was Jonn and Ivy. I. Must. Keep. Silent.

"Well?" he pressed.

I moved one hand helplessly, and his eyes dropped to it. He sighed quietly, and stepped back, facing the map.

"That is all. You may go."

At first I thought I'd misheard. "What?"

"Go," he said. "I am done with you for now. Bring me information, and you will not regret it."

I fled for the door.

FOURTEEN

I EMERGED FROM the building and staggered for the street. My thoughts turned anxious somersaults in my head. My hands shook.

He'd been in the midst of an interrogation, and then he'd withdrawn and let me go. I didn't know what had caused his abrupt change in mood, but I wasn't going to wait around in case he decided it'd been a mistake. I ducked down a canyon of stone between two shops and huddled against the wall, struggling to breathe as I tried to calm myself. My thoughts spiraled in my head. Ann had betrayed me. I'd been singled out for questioning— and then let go. Korr was looking for Echlos...

Korr was looking for Echlos.

A single shard of dread lodged itself in my chest.

The map.

Ann's father had a map in his study that marked the place. It had belonged to my parents and it had been stolen by Cole from their bodies after they'd died. The map was only half of what was needed to find the location, but it was more than I wanted Korr to have.

With it, he could still find Echlos if he was clever enough. And the man was clever enough.

"Lia?"

Strong arms caught me, and I smelled pine as a cloak enveloped me. *Adam?* What—how— But I didn't think further, didn't hesitate. I folded into him as he pulled me close. His cloak was heavy and warm around my shoulders. His hands brushed over my hair, my cheeks. His eyes sought mine, and I read the panic in them. "Are you hurt? Did he hurt you?"

How had he known? Who had told him?

"Lia?" A note of panic split his voice.

I shook my head, and he exhaled in relief.

"I heard you'd been taken," he said.

Children ran past us, and a pair of girls in snow-white cloaks hurried by the entrance to the alley. We broke apart dizzily, and Adam took me by the arm and drew me deeper into the shadows. As soon as we were out of sight, he dropped his hand and stepped back. He ran both hands through his hair and bit his lip. When he spoke, his voice was barely audible. "He interrogated you?"

It was cold without him close. My senses were spinning...Korr, the interrogation, Adam... Everything was in a jumble. I couldn't think straight. I rubbed my arms and gulped air to clear my head. The wind swirled around us, teasing the edges of our cloaks and tugging at our hair. Adam's thick curls blew into his eyes and across his cheeks.

"I didn't say anything," I whispered. "But he mentioned Echlos."

Adam's face turned ashen. "Are you certain?"

"I'm certain."

He scowled. "He's here to find the PLD. I'm sure of it."

Why did they want this device so badly? What did it do? "Well, then we have to find it first."

"We need more time."

I bit my lip. "Adam, the map in the Mayor's study. It mentions Echlos. What if he sees it?"

We stared at each other.

"We have to get that map," he said. He began to pace, his head lowered and his arms crossed. Finally he whirled to face me.

"The map is in the Mayor's study. I can't go near the house, but you have an invitation to the Elders' gathering. So you are going to get to the map."

"If by 'invitation' you mean working as a servant—"

"It's a way in," he said.

"But how am I supposed to get into the Mayor's study?"

He studied me. "You did it before."

Before, yes. When I still could trust my best friend. When everything was simpler. When at least I knew who my enemies were. "I can't ask Ann for help. She betrayed me, Adam."

A spark of something I couldn't define glimmered in his eyes. "Don't be so quick to burn that bridge. She might have had a reason."

I didn't know how to reply to that.

"When are you supposed to help Ann?" he asked

"Tomorrow night." Fresh apprehension squeezed in my chest. Could I do it now? Could I face her? Could I face Korr?

"Perfect. Find a way to get to the map, and we'll meet afterward."

"Is there any way you might be able to get into the study without Ann's help?"

"I'd have to find the key," I said. "I think the Mayor carries it on his person."

"You'll be serving, yes?"

"I think so." Ann hadn't really explained what the extent of my duties would be.

"Well," he mused, "there may be more than one copy. And if you can't find one, you could always pick the lock."

"I don't know how to pick locks!"

"It's not too difficult. I'll teach you."

"I don't know—"

Footsteps echoed at the end of the alley. Adam stepped back. "We'll make more plans tonight," he said quietly. "You can do this; don't worry."

And then he was gone.

I headed for the gate to the Frost slowly, my head still spinning from everything that had happened.

As I passed the quota yard, a flicker of red caught my eye.

Ann.

She stood in the shadows of the Assembly Hall, her arms wrapped tight around her waist as if she was physically holding herself together. Her face was the

178

color of fresh snow, and dark circles ringed her eyes. When she caught sight of me, the pinch in her shoulders eased, and she leaned back against the corner of the building as if she'd suddenly lost all the strength in her legs.

I kept walking. I passed her and I didn't stop.

I didn't miss the expressions that flitted across her face—pain, sadness, guilt.

I reached the gate and didn't look back.

~

Adam met me at the barn before dusk descended. He'd brought a lock and a handful of slender metal picks along with him, and he spread the tools on the barn floor for me to see.

"If you can't find the key," he said, "you'll have to use this. It's really very simple."

It didn't look simple, but I wasn't going to let a little scrap of metal defeat me. I watched carefully as Adam picked up the longest, thinnest pick and inserted it into the lock. He explained the mechanisms, and then I tried it. I struggled, and he covered my fingers with his.

"No, like this."

I went still, shocked by the warmth of his hand. A prickle ran up my arm.

He let go of me and sat back, letting me try again.

Finally, I succeeded in opening the lock.

"Good," Adam said, clearly pleased. "You did well."

"But what if I can't do it tomorrow? What if I forget, or panic?"

"You're one of the calmest, smartest people I know," he said. "You aren't going to forget. You aren't going to panic. And besides, you are probably going to find the key. This is just a backup plan."

You're one of the calmest, smartest people I know. I gaped at him. Compliments were not easy to come by from Adam Brewer, but this was the third time he'd given me one in as many weeks.

He looked at me, and I schooled my features into a somber expression. I didn't want him to see my confusion.

There was so much to sort out in my head.

~

The next day, I made the journey into town. The streets seemed emptier of villagers and fuller of soldiers. Had more Farthers come? Where were all the townsfolk?

My attention focused on the quota yard, where a small crowd had gathered. A few people were crying. Apprehension filled my veins, and I stepped closer to try to see what was going on. Had the Watchers gotten another Fisher?

Footsteps crunched in the snow behind me. I turned. Leon, the blacksmith's son.

"This is what happens when we don't fight back," he said, nodding at the crowd.

"What happened?" I asked.

He turned his pale gaze on me. "One of the Tailors resisted when the soldiers tried to take his quota. He's been arrested and sent away."

Another arrest. Another story of injustice.

"We are going to do something about this nonsense," he said. "We have a plan."

Their chaotic anger frightened me almost as much as the Farthers' capricious cruelty. I sucked in a breath. "What are you going to do?"

"If you wanted to know, you shouldn't have refused to join us." And then he pushed his way through the crowd, leaving me standing alone. The wind swept over me, teasing the edges of my cloak and numbing my cheeks.

A hand touched my arm, and I jumped.

Ann.

Had she seen me talking to Leon? Would she think anything of it?

We stared at each other. A thousand things simmered on my tongue, but I didn't know how to say the words. My eyes burned, and my throat felt tight.

"The Elders' gathering..." she said finally, making a useless gesture with one hand. "I thought perhaps you'd forgotten. But here you are."

I managed a curt nod. She bit her lip and motioned for me to follow her, and together we began to walk in the direction of the Mayor's house.

"Lia," she began.

"Don't," I said sharply.

She dropped her head and didn't say anything else.

We made the trip to the house in silence.

Villagers passed us in the streets. News of the arrest seemed to have spread. Their mouths were set in grim lines, and their eyes shifted from face to face. Everyone drew away from Ann as if she were diseased, and a few threw suspicious glances my way too. More than once I heard a whispered hiss—"Traitor!"

Ann walked with her head high and her back straight, although she flinched at the accusation.

I didn't know what to feel anymore.

We reached the Mayor's house and climbed the long flight of steps to the porch. Colored lanterns threw pools of violet and pink light across our path and made the trees in the garden glow. A servant rushed to open the door, and another took our cloaks as we swept inside. Warmth and light enveloped us as we moved through the foyer.

My eyes passed over the finery—crisp paper covered the walls, and a chandelier glittered above our heads. The house seemed even finer than the last time I'd been here. Every inch of the floors and carved furniture gleamed.

Several members of the Elder families hovered in the foyer, their cheeks pale and their shoulders stiff. I recognized them all, but I'd never spoken to most of them in my life. A Weaver and an Elder had little reason to mingle socially. But now we were all fish in the same bucket, as my father would say.

Ann brushed past them for the hall to speak to a servant, but I stopped by the staircase. My gaze strayed up it. I needed to get into the Mayor's study to find my parents' map, but how? Surely it was locked. And I could not ask Ann for help.

The sensation of being unable to trust my best friend felt like a knife in my chest.

"Lia Weaver?" a voice asked at my elbow.

I turned. A wide-eyed young man—Kirth Elder, I remembered—watched me. I gave him a wary look, half-relieved to make conversation and half-worried at what he'd say. "Yes?"

He might have been wondering what I'd done to be invited to such an auspicious gathering, but he only whispered, "Do I look as frightened as you do right now?"

"Maybe," I muttered, less pleased at his observation.

"This whole charade is madness," he said bitterly. "Dining with the Farther boots that grind us into the dirt?"

"And yet here you are," I said.

Ann reappeared. "Let me show you to the kitchen, Lia."

I followed her silently down the hall and into a vast, paneled room. Windows of stained glass let in streams of amber light, and a long oak table carved with snow blossoms and depictions of twisted tree branches filled the middle of the space. I'd never been in this part of the house before, and I gaped at the finery.

183

"The guests will dine in here," she said, avoiding my eyes. "You'll be in charge of serving food and filling glasses. I have a uniform for you in the kitchen pantry, and you can leave your clothes and cloak in the servants' room."

We exited the dining hall and entered a small corridor that led to the kitchen. Gleaming metal stoves and a massive hearth glowed with heat, and pots belched steam into the air. Ann found my uniform and handed it to me.

"When you're finished," she said, "you'll receive your payment. Sugar, salt, and flour, and any leftovers from the meal you can carry."

I eyed the platters of smoked fish and baked lemon pie, and my stomach pinched with hunger. I nodded.

She excused herself, and I found a closet and tugged on the uniform. There were no pockets, so I slid the lock picks Adam had given me into my braid as if they were hairpins. I returned to the kitchen.

A cook with cheeks red from the heat shoved a pitcher at me. "Fill the glasses," she barked, gesturing toward the dining hall.

I swallowed a retort and headed back down the servants' corridor. The pitcher was heavy in my hands. My boots made a smacking sound against the floor.

Music began to drift from the corner, where a trio of players plucked at the strings of a wind harp and played wood flutes. The soothing sounds did little to soothe me. In fact, the music seemed to mock my panic.

I drew in a deep breath and let it out, trying to stay calm. I began to fill the glasses as I glanced around the room.

I had to try to find that key to the study.

Where was the Mayor?

The doors opened, and servants scurried forward to hold them wide as the guests of honor entered the room.

The Elder families came first, walking carefully as if they were treading on broken glass. Officer Raine entered the room behind them, limping. He was followed by Korr, who slunk into the room with the grace of a cat. His gaze trailed over every face in the room and landed on mine. He smiled faintly, predatorily. I froze, my fingers curling stiffly around the pitcher, and then I rushed to finish my task so I could escape his notice.

A movement at my elbow startled me, and Ann took her place at the chair beside me. We didn't look at each other, but I felt the knowledge of her presence seep into my awareness.

The Mayor entered last and spread his hands to indicate the table. "Please sit, everyone."

The scraping of chairs filled the room. Raine took his place at the head of the table, near the Mayor, but Korr drifted down the length of the table and drew out a chair across from Ann. She stiffened. My stomach twisted into a hard knot, and I dropped my gaze to the table as my heartbeat beat staccato in my ears.

"Ladies," Korr drawled, dropping into the chair and picking up his napkin. He looked at me and then at his empty glass. When I filled the glass, he picked it up and studied the contents as if he couldn't decide whether or not he wanted to drink them. He smiled, and the corner of his cheek dimpled. "You betray your feelings too easily, Annalise."

Ann sat stiffly, her jaw clenched. A faint pink rose in her cheeks, and her shoulders twitched at the use of her full name.

I lifted my eyebrows. His attention was focused on Ann with the precision and intensity of a stonecutter chiseling away at a block of marble.

"You're far from your Aeralian compatriots," Ann said. Her voice was both sharp and breathless, as if her throat had tightened. "It's unseemly—"

"What's unseemly," Korr interrupted, setting down his glass with a thump and leaning across the table, "is the coldness with which you've treated me. I'm a guest in your father's house, and yet you barely speak to me."

Her hand trembled when she reached for her knife, but she lifted her chin. "Raine will be angry if you sit here. He's looking at you like he wants to rip your head off."

"He always wants to rip everyone's head off," Korr said carelessly. "It's his reason for existence." Nevertheless, Korr cut a glance at the officer, who was glowering from his place. He sighed and flicked an eyebrow at her. "Save a dance for me, Annalise," he said with a smirk, and pushed back his chair to stand.

She let out her breath as soon as he'd moved out of earshot and pressed a hand over her eyes.

186

I sat silent, still absorbing the exchange. Ann bit her lip and fiddled with her napkin. Suddenly she bent forward, reaching for her cup. As her fingers closed around it, she turned her head and her lips brushed my hair. "Lia," she whispered. "I must speak with you privately later, after the dinner is finished. Meet me in the hall when they begin the dancing." Louder, she said, "This glass is dirty. Bring me a new one, please."

I took the glass and returned it to the kitchen. My face was stoic, but inside I felt as if I were being pulled into pieces. Give her a chance to explain, or not? She'd betrayed me. She'd shattered my trust. But...it was *Ann*.

We began to serve the meal. I carried platters of fish and trays of nutbread and berry crème tarts from the kitchen and laid them on the table. Officer Raine reached for a tart right off the tray I held. He put the whole thing in his mouth, and crumbs fell onto his jacket.

Korr watched as if looking for my reaction, but when I gave none, he smirked and whispered something in the Mayor's ear.

At the other end of the table, Ann watched me too.

Unease gnawed at me, and the lilting music from the corner plucked at my nerves like restless fingers. The key. The Map. Korr. Ann.

"Officer Raine," Korr drawled. "Tell me about this problem you've been having with the local monsters."

Raine's lips thinned. He brushed his fingers on a napkin. "No problems," he said. "Minor mishaps, perhaps, but nothing that can't be fixed with some discipline."

Mishaps? Was that what he called it? My blood simmered, and I had to clamp my mouth shut to keep from protesting. People were *dead.*

Korr leaned back in his chair and smirked at the officer. "What are you going to do, build more fences to keep them out? It doesn't seem to be working."

Raine's face began to turn purple. "It's a complicated matter."

"And these malcontents I've been hearing about?"

Raine's brow wrinkled. "Malcontents?"

"I don't know what you call them," Korr said, waving a hand. "They call themselves Blackcoats, or so I've heard. The whole town is buzzing about them and the messages they've been leaving on walls. Particularly your walls."

"My men are dealing with it," Raine said. He reached for his wine and took a gulp.

Korr laced both hands behind his head. "I hope they do. I wouldn't want to have to give his Lordship the Emperor a bad report."

Raine set his glass down hard. He looked ready to explode.

"Gentlemen," the Mayor interrupted with an anxious smile, "I believe the meal is almost finished, but there will be dancing."

Korr looked at Ann. She looked at me.

I returned to the kitchen, my mind churning. Ann still needed to speak with me. I still needed to find a way to get into the study.

The dinner dragged on. The Elder families muttered politely, Korr smirked, and Raine glowered. The Mayor looked ill. Ann stared at a point on the wall and ate without speaking. The mood in the room was as chilly as the mountain winds, but everyone pretended otherwise.

Finally, we began to clear away the plates. Servants began to dismantle the table, clearing the room, and the musicians stopped to fiddle with their instruments. The music began to play again, and a few of the younger Elder family members paired off. I watched unobtrusively from the wall with the rest of the servants.

Raine and Korr appeared to be arguing by their body posture, although their faces were flat and composed. After a moment, Korr broke away and approached Ann.

"I believe you promised me a dance?" he said to her with another dimpled smirk.

Ann gritted her teeth, accepted his outstretched hand, and let him draw her into the center of the room.

I shot a glance toward the doorway. Down the hall, up the stairs and to the left was the Mayor's study. I could slip away without anyone noticing if I did it now, while they were all occupied.

But I needed the key. But where was it?

The Mayor stood by Raine, watching the dancers and sipping from his drink. He wore no coat to keep a key in. My gaze traveled back to the chairs that had been moved against the walls.

His coat lay across two of them. An Aeralian-style jacket, with pockets.

I headed for the chairs slowly, deliberately.

No one was looking.

My fingers touched the edge of the first pocket, and my heartbeat quickened. I dipped into the pocket with my hand as I shifted my position on the chair. Voices hummed around me. The music swelled. One of the dancers giggled nervously. My fingers brushed the bottom of the pocket.

Nothing.

Gently, I withdrew my hand and stole a glance around the room. Ann and Korr were still occupied. Raine was still speaking quietly with the Mayor. The rest of the Elder families were either dancing or standing together in clumps, glasses clutched in their hands and thin smiles fixed politely on their faces.

I reached for the second pocket, moving my hand in increments across the folded fabric. My pulse hummed. I couldn't breathe. My skin prickled with the awareness that at any moment, someone could turn and see me.

I couldn't quite reach inside, not without bending over...

I pulled out one of my hairpins and let it fall to the floor. As I leaned over to pick it up, I slid my hand into the second pocket. Cold metal met my fingertips.

The key.

I stood back up slowly, folding the key into my hand as I breathed out and looked around.

I'd done it. Now I just needed to get to the study and find the map.

The song ended, and the couples drew apart. Ann made a beeline for me. I kept my hand with the key closed, because I had no pockets in my dress in which to hide it. She stopped by my chair and lowered her voice as her eyes darted around the room.

"We need to talk now. Please."

A perfect reason to leave the room. I let her lead me into the hall and through the foyer. I tried not to look too longingly at the stairs as we passed them. We stepped into a servants' hallway that opened off the main level, and Ann shut the door behind us. It was all so familiar, and yet so backward from the last party I'd been at in this house.

She turned to me, eyes downcast. She drew in a deep breath. "Lia... I don't know what to say."

I waited. A mixture of emotions rose in my chest—the betrayal I felt, along with the memory of Adam's words and what I'd witnessed earlier. "Why?" I asked after a pause.

Sadness pooled in her eyes. "I can't explain everything right now. I wish I could. Please believe me— I didn't want to let him question you. But I had no choice!"

"I understand," I said, and I meant it. I knew what desperation felt like.

She shook her head. "But you won't forgive me?"

A sigh welled in my lungs and hissed from my lips. I could only be honest with her. "Ask me again in a few weeks."

She nodded and reached for the door. A tear slipped down her cheek, and she didn't even try to wipe it away. "We should get back."

My chest tightened. The key burned in my hand.

This was my moment.

Instead of following Ann down the hall toward the dining room, I hesitated by the stairs. She was hurrying so fast she didn't notice that I hadn't accompanied her, and I watched until she'd slipped through the doors before I turned to gaze up at the landing of the second floor. The steps of polish oak gleamed in the lamplight. They beckoned me. I threw a glance over my shoulder to make sure the foyer was empty. No servants or guest were in sight.

My feet whispered against the wood as I ascended the stairs. My heart pounded with every step. My palms tingled. In my head, I rehearsed my excuses if anyone caught me—I was looking for Ann, I had to borrow something I left in the room, I was lost. They all sounded laughably false to me.

Better not get caught, then.

I reached the landing and paused. A corridor lined with portraits led right and left—right to the Mayor's study, left to Ann's room. I went right.

Darkness lingered in this part of the house. The gas lamps flickered low in their sockets, and no windows let in any glimmer of the sunset. I moved carefully, quietly.

When I reached the corner, I held my breath and listened for the footsteps of a servant or guard. But I heard nothing.

I turned the corner and saw the door to the Mayor's study. My heart pounded, and perspiration broke out across my palms. I grasped the key tightly between my fingers and inserted it into the lock. I heard the soft click, and I pushed the door open.

A boom shook the house. Energy rippled through me, and heat singed my hair as the Mayor's study exploded in flames.

FIFTEEN

THE EXPLOSION THREW me back against the far wall. Pain ripped through my head and neck. I tasted blood. My ears were ringing.

Smoke poured through the open door, and I saw the dull gleam of flames rising from the Mayor's desk.

Had someone set a *bomb?*

The Blackcoats. I was sure of it.

I scrambled up and snatched the key from the lock. It was too hot to go inside. Surely the map was incinerated by now.

The smoke burned my lungs and reduced me to a coughing fit. I found the wall with my hand and forged ahead blindly as my lungs heaved and water streamed from my eyes.

Smoke was pouring down the stairs and filling the foyer by the time I reached the landing. Guests stumbled from the dining hall, coughing, and Farther soldiers rushed inside with their weapons drawn.

No one had noticed me at the stairs. I made a sweep of the room, but everything was in chaos and nobody was paying me any attention. Ann shouted orders as people streamed toward the exits. Lifting my skirt, I darted down the steps and joined the people leaving the house.

Outside, Officer Raine shouted orders while the Mayor paced. The Elder families lingered at a distance like a herd of startled deer, as if they didn't know whether to stay or slip away into the gathering dusk.

My lungs burned from the smoke, and I doubled over coughing. I hacked until I saw stars, and when I finally straightened the yard had filled with people whispering and pointing at the flames and smoke pouring from the second story of the house. I swept the group with my gaze. Where was Ann?

I scanned the yard for her, but saw no sign of her bright blonde hair. Suddenly my chest was squeezing and my stomach was twisting.

"Ann!" I screamed.

I ran back for the door, but before I reached it a booted foot kicked it open, and Korr emerged carrying Ann in his arms.

"Oh," I gasped, stepping aside. He carried her to the snow and set her down gently. Her cheeks were pale, and she bent over coughing after her feet touched the ground.

Korr straightened, keeping one hand on Ann's arm to steady her. His dark hair stirred in the wind as he gazed up at the second story of the house, where smoke streamed from the shattered window of the study, and his eyes narrowed in a squint as he turned his gaze on the rest of us as if looking for a culprit.

"Do your men have this under control, too?" he asked Raine in a low, furious voice. It was the first time I'd seen him truly angry.

He thought it was the Blackcoats, too.

I remembered the key in my hand. I didn't need it now. I uncurled my fingers and let it fall into the snow beneath a bush.

If they found it on me, they'd suspect me.

The evening was startlingly cold, and I didn't have my cloak. I shivered in the wind as Raine and Korr exchanged angry words in heated whispers.

Ann glanced in my direction but didn't move toward me. The expression on her face told me to go, and so I did, slipping through the garden and toward the center of the village. I tucked my numb fingers under my arms and ran to warm myself as my mind swam with questions.

Had the Blackcoats set fire to the Mayor's study? It had to have been them. Was this their way of demonstrating that the people of the village were not as happy about the occupation? Or had they been trying to injure Officer Raine, the Mayor, Ann?

Surely their trap was for the Mayor. Who else would have been injured if the bomb was set to detonate when the door was opened?

My head ached along with my smoke-stung lungs. My thoughts swirled like frightened birds. I struggled to focus.

Adam was waiting at the quota yard. I needed to find him.

I reached the center of the village, where villagers had already begun to gather and point at the column of smoke rising from the Mayor's house at the top of the hill. I sank into the shadows, avoiding everyone's gaze. Where was Adam?

A shadow detached from a doorway and slid toward me. Adam. I continued walking until I reached an alley, and then I slipped into the darkness and waited.

He leaned against the wall beside me. "Well?"

Breathlessly, I explained what had happened.

He listened without interrupting, his gaze intent on my face. The only movement he made was to remove his cloak and drop it over my shoulders when he saw I'd lost mine. I burrowed into the soft folds gratefully and concluded by saying, "I think it may have been the Blackcoats."

"You may be right," he mused. "But I did not think they were so clever as to plant a bomb in the Mayor's locked study. Were they trying to send a message to the Aerialans, or injure the Mayor and his family?"

"I wondered the same thing," I said. "Leon told me only hours ago that they had plans. This must have been it."

"Either way, this is good for us," he said. "It buys us time. The map has been destroyed, surely, and the Farthers are going to be focusing on catching the culprits rather than worrying about any residual Thorns influence. Now go home, Lia Weaver, before the Watchers slither out of the woods."

"What about you?" I asked.

"I'll be fine. I have things to do still."

"I can help."

"You can help by making sure your siblings are all right. Go home, please."

I didn't remember that I had his cloak until he was already gone.

SIXTEEN

I PUT AWAY Ann's servant uniform and Adam's cloak and tugged on one of my woolen nightgowns as soon as I got back to the house. Ivy was asleep in her bed, her arms thrown above her head, her body curled into a contorted shape. The rise and fall of her chest comforted me, and I lingered by her pillow to watch her sleep for a few minutes before descending the stairs to the main room.

Jonn waited by the fire. The light from the fire licked at his face and made shadows around his eyes and mouth. He didn't turn to look at me, but I felt his attention all the same. I paused at the bottom of the stairs, and a million unspoken words crowded into my mouth.

Jonn was my brother. We'd been through everything together, and he'd been one of my closest confidants once. Now we were barely speaking, and Ann and I were practically estranged. The pressure of having everyone I loved gone or angry or untrustworthy felt like a pile of stones strapped to my back. I sighed. What should I do?

He turned his head. "You came home in Adam's cloak." It was a statement and a question.

"I lost mine," I said, and then I hesitated. The truth of what had happened was so huge, so overwhelming. "Someone blew up the Mayor's study, and we had to evacuate the house."

"A bomb?"

I sank into a chair and rubbed my eyes. "Some sort of crude explosive device. Smoke was everywhere. I hit my head... The whole party had to evacuate into the snow." I stared off into space. Details kept striking me, little things. The way Korr had carried Ann, as if she were made of glass. The column of smoke leaking into the sky from the top of the house. The way Adam's eyes had softened ever so slightly when he'd given me his cloak. "I left my cloak behind at the Mayor's house. It's probably lost now."

"Do you think the whole house will burn?" Jonn asked.

"I...maybe not." Raine's men would put it out, perhaps. I thought of Ann, with no place to go and night falling. Where would she stay?

"You should use one of Ma's," he said, still talking about my cloak.

"Good idea," I said, still thinking of Ann. Was she all alone tonight? Surely her father would make sure she was all right. But she had no siblings to care for her, not the way I did. I lifted my gaze to my brother, and found him watching me.

"Lia," he said, and stopped. His face crumpled.

Something in my chest loosened. My throat squeezed up with tears, and we looked at each other, and then we were both talking at once.

"I'm so sorry—"

"I can't do this—"

We laughed shakily together, and some of the tension in my chest turned into hopefulness. "You first," I said.

He rubbed a hand through his hair. "No, you."

"All right." I breathed in deeply, choosing my words carefully. "I am so sorry about what I said to you. I'm sorry if I ever gave you the impression that I don't need you. I do need you. I'm about to break. I've got nobody to lean on and nowhere to turn, and everything is going wrong. I need my brother."

"I can help you," he said.

I nodded. My throat felt tight, and my eyes burned, but I didn't cry. I wasn't a crier. When he smiled hesitantly at me, the room felt lighter and warmer. I crossed to the fire and perched in the chair beside him. "All right," I said.

"All right?"

We'd said nothing and everything. I didn't know where this left us, but somehow a breach had been healed. I breathed easier, my chest felt lighter and my mouth curved in an involuntary smile of pure relief.

I had him back.

"No more secrets," I promised. "Not from you."

"Well, then." He leaned forward and braced his elbows against his knees. "Tell me what you've been up to."

Jonn listened thoughtfully as I poured out a description of our travels to Echlos and our search for the mysterious device. His forehead wrinkled as I talked about the documents we'd searched, and he chewed his lip but didn't ask questions or interrupt. When I'd finished, he leaned back and stared at the fire.

"What?" I demanded finally, when I couldn't stand it any longer. "What are you thinking?"

He tipped his head to the side, his eyes unfocused and thoughtful. "Our parents knew about this, I think."

I didn't remember Adam mentioning it. "Why do you say that?"

"They have a history with Echlos. Da wrote about it in his journals. If this thing is important, and Adam Brewer thinks he can find information to its location in a bunch of old documents, then I think our parents might have something about it in one of their papers."

I considered this. It made sense. "All right," I said. "So we look through their things."

He stared hard at the flames. He swallowed hard. "And if I find it, you'll let me join the Thorns?"

"I—it's not up to me."

"Promise me, Lia." His voice was suddenly fierce. "I can't be useless like this forever."

"You aren't useless."

He speared me with an exasperated look.

"I'll talk to Adam," I conceded. "But I can't promise…"

"It makes sense for me to be involved," he argued. "Our parents worked as a team before, didn't they? Why can't we take their place together? I already know about the Thorns, and I live in this house, too."

"It does make sense," I admitted. "But Adam's unpredictable. I don't know what he'll say."

"I think he'll say yes, if you're asking," Jonn said.

I paused. "Why do you say that?"

"Never mind." He reached for the yarn basket beside his chair, but I snagged his wrist and squeezed, dragging his attention back to me.

"Why?"

"It's nothing. It was a careless remark. You and Adam are friends, that's all."

"Well," I breathed, leaning back and letting go. "I suppose we are."

But when I climbed the steps to my bedroom later, an uncomfortable feeling gnawed at me.

Just friends.

Was it true?

~

Jonn threw himself into the search, and the light was still glowing under the door of our parents' room when I rose to do the morning chores. I knocked softly and found him sitting on the floor with stacks of journals and maps surrounding him.

"Any luck?"

"I found something," he said. "A mention, not a location."

"Well, that means we might be on the right track," I said. "A mention means they know about it. Can I see?"

He held the paper out wordlessly, and I scanned my father's scrawl. "We have hidden the PLD," I read, and inhaled sharply. I looked from the page to my brother's exhausted face. "Does he say where?"

"No," he muttered. "I've looked through everything. He doesn't mention it again."

"I'll tell Adam. He'll want to know. And Jonn…"

He rubbed his face with his knuckles. "Yes?"

"Get some sleep before Ivy wakes up."

~

Adam found me in the barn.

"Lia Weaver," he said quietly from beside my elbow.

I almost dropped the bucket of feed I'd been filling. "*Adam.* You have to stop doing that."

"Sorry." A smile hovered around his mouth and sparkled in his eyes, a rare show of humor for him. "Maybe you should learn to listen better."

"I can't help it if you walk like a ghost." I pushed past him to get to the horses, irritable but only a little bit. I was mostly teasing. "And you enjoy startling me. Don't think I don't know it."

He followed, and I heard him chuckle under his breath. "I see you made it home safely?"

"Yes. I ran the whole way. Thank you for your cloak, by the way. Did you freeze?"

"I found another," he said lightly, brushing my concern away.

"I have something to tell you."

Adam raised both eyebrows and leaned back against the stall door, watching me without comment.

"I...told Jonn about the PLD."

He gazed at me steadily and didn't speak.

"I thought it was a good idea," I continued, rushing on. "He already knew about the Thorns, and my parents were a team, and we've found some things of theirs that mentioned the device..."

"What? You found mention of it?"

"Yes—wait—you aren't mad about me involving Jonn?"

"Jonn is intelligent and determined. He'll make a great addition, and I've always expected he'd someday be incorporated," Adam said quickly. "Now tell me more about this mention."

I told him what I knew, which wasn't much. "Do you think they hid it somewhere in Echlos, or somewhere else?" I glanced around the barn. "Here?"

"Maybe," he said. "And you're sure there was nothing else? Not even a hint?"

"Nothing. Jonn's been reading through my da's journals all night. But there's still more to look through." I hesitated, looking around the room. "We should search the secret room, maybe. Look through all the boxes."

"Good idea."

A puff of musty air wafted up from the darkness when I opened the trap door. Adam grabbed a lantern from the hook by the horse stalls and joined me. We descended the steep staircase into the gloom, and the scent of old papers and crumbling dirt enveloped me.

When we reached the bottom, he grabbed a stack of boxes from the top shelf, which Jonn and Ivy hadn't touched. We settled on the floor and started shuffling through them. I stole a few glances at him, trying to see what he might be thinking about this new development. But his expression was unreadable as usual.

Silence enveloped us.

I cast about for something else to say. "Do you think the Watchers have been creeping around the town at night regularly now?"

"Maybe. Traveling through the Frost has become even more perilous, as you saw the last time I showed up on your doorstep."

"Everything's become more perilous," I muttered. "The forest is full of Watchers and the village is full of Farthers, and both of them are breathing down our necks." I remembered something I'd heard the previous night. "Last night Korr threatened Raine with ramifications from the Aeralian Emperor if he didn't stop the attacks. Could he actually do something about what's going on in our village?"

Adam shook his head. "The only ones with power are the ones with the guns. Don't be fooled into thinking otherwise."

I bent over the box in front of me with renewed purpose as I considered his perspective on Aeralian political power. "If you're not Aeralian, then why are you with the Thorns?"

That question earned me another faint smile. "Why are you?"

"Because somebody had to do something."

He nudged my shoulder gently. "Well, we aren't so different, you and I."

SEVENTEEN

I AVOIDED THE village for days while Jonn and I searched our parents' archives for more mentions of the PLD. Ivy begged to take the quota, and I let her. She was restless, and we needed to keep her occupied while we worked.

We were running out of time.

On the fourth day after the explosion, I finally took a break from searching to check the traps in the forest. Tramping through the frozen wasteland seemed to clear my head, and it made me feel unexpectedly close to my father. I stood very still in the middle of the white wilderness, listening to the quiet sounds of melting snow and bluewing calls that echoed through the trees.

"Where is it, Da?" I whispered aloud.

The wind fanned my face, and I sighed. I checked the traps. We'd caught nothing. Dejected, I turned for home. I stopped by the barn to check the animals, and all was dark and quiet and safe. Before going into the house, I scanned the tree line, an old habit, although I didn't know if I was looking for Farthers, Watchers, or Blackcoats anymore.

Life had become a muddle of danger and disappointment.

My bones ached at the thought of another sleepless night, but we were no closer to finding the PLD than before, and Adam was growing increasingly anxious. He'd promised to come by the house and help us after Ivy was asleep, and so I'd agreed.

I knocked the snow from my boots and went inside. The fire crackled in the silence. The room was empty except for my brother, who sat in his chair with quota in his lap.

"Where's Ivy?"

Jonn looked up from the yarn. "I thought she was in the barn with you."

"No..." I covered my face with my hands and sighed. "Why can that girl not stay put for five seconds? Could she be upstairs?"

We listened together, and I heard no sign of movement overhead, but sometimes she fell asleep on her bed in the middle of the day. I climbed the staircase and counted the steps I took to calm my temper.

"Ivy?"

Shifting light and shadows poured through the window and pooled on the quilt of her bed. The room was empty.

A spiral of quiet panic twisted in my stomach, but I forced it down. I wasn't going to let myself be frightened, not yet. It was probably nothing. She was probably behind the house, talking to a baby bluewing and coaxing it out with berries.

It was fine. She was just outside. I repeated it to myself and some of the tension slipped from my shoulders.

As I turned to go, the glint of something caught my eye. I stopped.

What was that beneath her bed?

I crossed the room to her bed and crouched down. I reached under the bedframe, and my fingers brushed cold metal. *Just a lantern.* The squeeze in my chest eased, and I sat back on my heels as irritation took the place of panic. Was she trying to burn down the house by reading late at night again? Last time she'd fallen asleep and almost set her sheets on fire.

When I pulled the lantern out from under the bed it snagged on a piece of fabric. I reached back under and pulled out a black shirt. One of my father's shirts.

What...?

I got down on my hands and knees and yanked out everything crammed beneath the bed frame. A pair of black trousers. A pair of boots. A small black cloak.

I lifted them to the light with numb fingers. My hands shook. My stomach twisted. My mouth formed the word as fury filled me like fire, incinerating every single thought in my mind except the horrible, heavy knowledge of what this meant.

Blackcoats.

~

When I got to the village proper, I immediately knew something was amiss. The air felt heavy, clotted. Villagers hurried by with their heads lowered and their cloaks pulled tight. A few people stood in a knot around the Assembly Hall.

My heart jumped into my throat. Another death from Watchers? I pushed my way to the front and grabbed the arm of the person closest to me. "What's happened?" I demanded.

He glanced down. "Haven't you heard? Three young people have been arrested."

"Arrested?" My voice was breathless, shrill. I stepped back. "Why?"

"For setting fire to the Mayor's house. They've been detained as part of the investigation." He lowered his voice. "If they are found guilty, they'll be sent to Aeralian detention camps."

My head was spinning. I staggered back and leaned against the wall. Aeralian detention camps? It wasn't a hanging, but it was still a death sentence.

"W-who was arrested?" I asked, before the man could move on.

He shook his head. "I don't know the names, but they're being held at the consulate."

I ran.

Her name was a mindless chant in my mind—IvyIvyIvyIvyIvy—and I couldn't breathe, couldn't think beyond the churning sense of foreboding building in my veins. My cloak flowed behind me as I fled down the

211

street and turned the corner. The consulate gleamed ahead of me, cruel and cold in the sunlight. I ran faster.

I could see figures in the yard, beyond the pointed metal fence that separated the consulate from the street. The workers had finished it days ago. The ground around the building was broken and churned up, as if it had burrowed itself into the earth like a mole.

In front of the consulate building were three prisoners, their hands in chains.

I came to an abrupt stop, my heart racing and my breath coming in painful gasps. I scanned the figures.

My sister was not among them.

I staggered with relief.

The unhappy trio lifted their heads at my approach, and I inhaled sharply as the light fell on their faces. The first two were blond-haired boys who I didn't know, but...Kirth Elder?

"You," I said, astonished. "You are with the Blackcoats?"

He glared at me, defiant, and didn't answer.

He'd been at the Mayor's house the night of the explosion. Had he planted the bomb in the study?

It didn't matter. Right now, nothing mattered but my sister's safety.

I returned to the village square. If Ivy wasn't among the detainees, then where was she?

I searched the village for hours, and finally, I headed back home.

~

When Ivy came back, Jonn and I were waiting by the fire. The door slammed, and we looked at each other. I took a deep breath and faced my sister.

"Where have you been, Ivory Augusta Weaver?" I asked. My voice was tight and quiet, but she flinched as if I'd yelled.

"In the village." She tucked a strand of hair behind her ear and hunched her shoulders up around her neck.

"It isn't quota day. It isn't Assembly day."

She didn't say anything. I reached behind my back and pulled out the black shirt I'd found.

"What is this?"

Her face crumpled, but she lifted her chin. "Why were you going through my things?"

"Tell me this isn't what I think it is," I said. My previous rage had burned away everything in me but stony resolve. My voice was soft as ashes, and just as cold.

"Why were you going through my things?"

"Ivy," Jonn said. He spoke quietly, but it broke her. She began to cry. The sight of her tears ignited me again, and I rose to my feet.

"The threatening note in the barn?" I demanded. "Did you leave it?"

She pressed her lips together. Her eyes were shiny with tears. "I'm fighting back against the Farthers just like you."

"You're being stupid!" I shouted it. Fury licked at my insides like freshly stoked fire. My hands trembled.

Jonn put a hand on my arm, quieting me. "Ivy. You can't be part of the Blackcoats."

"Ma and Da—" she began.

"Ma and Da would never have let you get involved in anything like this," I snapped. "The Blackcoats are reckless. They hate people like Ann, and they would have loathed Gabe on the spot and wanted him killed. Not to mention the fact that their methods are stupid and reckless. Three of them were arrested today."

Her eyes widened at the word *arrested*, but she pressed on. "They're trying to do good, and they need me," she protested hotly. "You're both helping with the Thorns now, don't pretend you're not. You cut me out, but I wanted to help, too. So I am. In my own way."

Jonn and I exchanged glances.

"Didn't you hear me? People were arrested. They might be deported." I said.

"I've barely done anything!" she exploded. "Only left a stupid note and carried a few messages."

"Good. And that's all you're doing."

"But—"

"This discussion is over," I said.

Shaking her head, she ran past us for the stairs.

I pressed a hand over my eyes.

At least she was safe.

We started work on the yarn, and I made stew in the pot over the fire. By the time the sky outside had turned dark and the scent of the stew began to fill the house, Ivy made her way down the stairs, her feet dragging and her eyes rimmed with red. She didn't speak when she reached us, but she plopped down by the hearth and grabbed a snarl of yarn from Jonn's feet to wind into a ball.

I tried not to stare, but I couldn't hide my astonishment that she'd made an appearance.

"Quota's due," she muttered when she noticed my incredulousness. "I'm not a child anymore, Lia, in case you haven't noticed. I pay attention to these things now. I'm going to pull my weight around here just like everybody else."

Jonn and I blinked at each other. "Good," I said, too surprised to say much else, and resumed my work. I was afraid to say too much and mess it up.

She bent over her work, attacking the yarn with all the ferocity of her personality.

For what felt like an infinite stretch of time, no one spoke. Then, finally, Jonn nudged her with his foot. When she glanced up, he asked, "What wakes in darkness and sleeps in light, can't be touched or seen with the eyes, but still inflicts intense fright?"

She scowled, clearly upset and not yet ready to put her hurt aside, but still she played along and answered. "A Watcher."

"*Can't* be touched or seen with the eyes," he repeated.

Ivy bit her lip. Her face wrinkled as if she was about to declare she didn't know, but then she blinked and gave him the faintest, most grudging of smiles. "A nightmare?"

He grinned at her. "You're getting good at this."

215

She lifted one shoulder in a shrug, but she seemed a little bit pleased. The tension in the room eased slightly, and I felt infinitesimally lighter. We could do this. Jonn and Ivy and I...we could find some sort of path between the external dangers and the internal strife.

Jonn grabbed another bunch of yarn and started winding it. "And who, in his most fearful moment, is also most brave?"

"A bluewing?"

"I always thought it was a Frost dweller," I remarked. "Isn't that what Da said?"

"A lot of Da's riddles had more than one answer," he said with a shrug.

More than one answer...

My hands paused, and I raised my head. "Jonn."

He turned his head, his gaze questioning. "What's wrong?"

For a moment, I couldn't speak. My mind spun, and chills ran over my skin. "What woven secret will keep you warm?" I finally blurted.

Woven secret...

We locked eyes.

His mouth formed an O as he made the connection. "Do you think...?"

I scrambled for the bedroom without answering, and there it was, folded at the foot of the bed. My ma's Frost quilt. The one she'd wrapped me in as a little girl, the one she'd always used to point out our farm, the village, everything.

A woven secret?

My fingers trembled as I shook it out. The colorful stitched patterns unfolded to the floor, spilling the map of fabric everywhere. I ran my hands over the village, our farm, the paths...

"It must be here somewhere," I muttered aloud.

A shadow filled the doorway. Jonn, hobbling. "Lia?" His voice was high-pitched with excitement.

I gathered the quilt in my arms. "Come on. I need to leave out the lantern."

Ivy watched us, wide-eyed, as we dragged the quilt to the fireside.

"Ivy," I said. "I need you to hang a lantern on the tree at the edge of the forest. The one with the huge branch that hangs over the yard."

She rose mutely and went to take it from the nail by the door while I shook the quilt out again and bent over the folds. Jonn joined me.

"See anything?"

"Lia," Jonn said, in cheerful exasperation. "We've been looking at this quilt our entire lives. It's not going to be glaringly obvious at first glance."

"Right." I ran my fingers over the stitches slowly, scanning every inch. Here was the village. Here was the path, edged in blue ribbon for the snow blossom bushes lining it. Here was the black swath of cloth that represented the river between the Farthers and us. Here was the icy lake, represented by a cloudy gray swatch, and here was our little farm, with a pale square for the house and a darker one for the barn. Tiny gray stitches made a path of footprints to the barn. I traced them with

217

the tip of my finger as memories filled my mind. I'd pretended to walk that path with my fingers over and over as a little girl.

The footprints...

I turned my head, tracing the glimmer of gray thread with my eyes. The forest of the Frost was a patchwork of fabric pieces and embroidery, a colorful cacophony of browns, whites, and gray. The thread glimmered through it all, a special, almost silver thread that caught the light and painted a shimmering trail. It wove around the barn and to the tree line of the forest, around the branches and up the side of the quilt toward...

"What is this?"

A tiny, thin brown square of fabric sewn into the midst of the forest.

He squinted at it. "I don't know. I've never even noticed that before."

"Look!" Along the edge of the square, in tiny stitches, were the letters:

P

L

D.

I would never have seen them if I hadn't been holding the fabric an inch from my face. In fact, I might not have even noticed them then, that was how cunningly they were worked into the pattern of the quilt.

"Unbelievable," Jonn muttered. Wonder filled his voice. "It's been here this whole time. And what is that? Some kind of barn, a shed?"

I laughed shakily. "When Adam gets here, we'll follow this thread trail and find out, I suppose." I rubbed my hands over my tired eyes and leaned back. "A woven secret... They were telling us all along. I can't believe it. They planted the clues for us before we even knew we needed them."

I hugged the quilt to my chest, and just like the riddle promised, I felt warm.

EIGHTEEN

A KNOCK WOKE me while the light was still pale and bluish through the curtains. Ivy was still asleep, wrapped up in so many blankets that I could barely see her. Everything below was still. Jonn was sleeping, too.

I wrapped myself in my mother's cloak and went down to open the door.

It was Adam. He stood in the shadow of the stoop, his dark hair messed by the wind and his eyes tired but alert, scanning my face for any sign of anxiety or fear. "I saw the lantern. What—"

"We found it," I whispered.

His mouth snapped shut, and for a moment, he didn't move. He stared at me, immobile, and then he stepped forward and grabbed my shoulders. "What did you say?"

"We found the map to where my father hid the PLD. It was on a quilt my mother made, and the clue to it was in an old riddle he used to tell us as children."

Adam was very, very still, as if he was afraid to move and wake from a dream. Finally, he exhaled deeply. "Unbelievable."

"That's what Jonn said, too." I couldn't stop grinning. We'd done it. Jonn and I had helped the Thorns just like our parents.

"Can I see the quilt?"

I stepped aside to let him in. He removed his cloak and shook the snow off his boots, and I led him to the fireside where the blanket lay across Jonn's empty chair. Adam studied it carefully while I watched him. He examined every inch with the care of a craftsman examining a masterpiece.

"Clever," he murmured appreciatively under his breath, speaking half to me and half to himself. "Hide the answer right out in the open where no one is looking for it. Incredibly clever. And who would look for the map on a blanket? Certainly not someone like me. Any person wanting to find this besides you or your brother would fail, because they'd be searching through old papers and maps instead of listening to family riddles."

We studied the blanket together for a moment, wrapped in reverent silence until my stomach rumbled with hunger and I grabbed the kettle to warm over the fire. But in my excitement, I filled it too full. I sloshed water on the floor.

"Here," he said, taking it from me. "Let me help."

"Have you eaten?"

He shook his head.

I let him situate the kettle while I got out the bread and butter and the last of yesterday's eggs from the hole in the wall by the window where they kept cold. Adam hung the kettle and stirred up the coals until they spat flames again, and when I stepped back into the main room, I smothered a smile at the sight of him tending a hearth so cozily.

"What?" he asked without looking up.

"Nothing..." I said. "You just make a pretty housewife, that's all."

He lifted his head and returned my grin with one of his own, the first I'd seen in a long time. "I've done my share of household chores, Lia Weaver."

"You always call me that."

"Call you what?"

"My full name—Lia Weaver."

He turned his head away casually as he reached for the fire tongs to poke the coals again. "Lia." The word was quiet, almost a caress, and for some reason hearing it made my stomach knot. I busied myself with the bread to hide how he'd flustered me.

"There's something else you should know," he said after a moment of silence.

I lifted my head and waited for him to continue.

"Some Blackcoat fools were arrested yesterday," Adam said. "Korr is saying he'll release them if anyone brings him information on Echlos, or a mysterious device connected with it."

All the breath left my lungs. "The PLD?"

Adam nodded.

I twisted my hands together. "What are we going to do?"

"Nothing," he said firmly.

I bit my lip hard. The voice of the man from yesterday echoed in my mind. "They'll be sent to detention camps—"

"We cannot give it up," he said. "Lives are depending on this device, Lia. The Blackcoats made their own decision."

"But—"

"We can't." He said it gently, firmly.

We stared at each other, and I saw he was as stricken as I was.

The door to my parents' bedroom opened, and Jonn limped out. "Brewer," he said, not sounding surprised to see him.

"Weaver," Adam replied evenly, tucking away his sadness with one blink.

I left them sizing each other up and retrieved the bread. I sliced it, buttered it, and brought it to the fire.

When I returned, Jonn and Adam were deep in a discussion about the best way to access the location indicated on the quilt-map. "I know this trail," Jonn said, tapping the line of silver thread. "My father used to use it to set his traps. It's an old deer run, and it's hard to follow because it constantly breaks and diverts and doubles back. Only our family knows the way."

"When do we leave?" I asked, my stomach suddenly a riot of nervousness and excitement.

Adam smiled with half his mouth. "How soon can you be ready?"

~

We left immediately. Ivy was still asleep, and Jonn was working on quota when we exited. Adam started toward the barn, but I called him back.

"The horses won't fit on the path. It's too narrow, too twisting." I hesitated. "Can we carry the PLD ourselves?"

Adam nodded. "Yes. All right then. On foot."

We entered the woods at the break in the trees just beyond the barn. The hush enveloped us, and the weird blue light filtering through the branches cast a chill across my skin. But I felt strong and warm in my mother's cloak. The snow blossoms bounced around my neck, reassuring me, and Adam strode beside me with his own cloak fluttering next to mine in the wind.

The only sound was the crunch of our footsteps and the hiss of our breath. The air was so cold it made my teeth ache. My fingers felt brittle even inside my thick wool gloves, and I tucked my hands under my arms to warm them. Around us, the Frost crackled with ice and shadowy silence.

"Did your father used to take you on this path?" Adam asked in a low voice, when we'd walked for some time. The warmth of his voice thawed me a little.

"Sometimes. He set traps along this path. He said it was a Weaver secret, a secret to be kept only in the family. He didn't want the villagers knowing he walked the deep Frosts." I paused, remembering. "He was never afraid to go into the Frost, you see."

"I remember," he said. "Your father was a brave man."

A hot itch that felt like tears started behind my eyes. "He was the bravest man I knew. My mother didn't walk the forests much, and never without him, but she was brave too. They were both so strong in the face of such hardship."

"As are you."

We glanced at each other, and words rustled in my throat, unspoken words I didn't even know how to say. A bluewing fluttered in the air above us, shattering the moment, and we pressed on while my heart beat fast and my blood tingled.

Our feet beat a desperate rhythm over the hard-packed earth. The trail made a damp ribbon of dark brown through the snow, weaving beneath trees and around rocks as deftly as my mother's stitches. We moved faster as the gloom deepened. Above our heads, clouds rolled in.

"Storm's coming," I said.

"We have a few hours still," he guessed, staring hard at a visible patch of sky when we paused to rest. "How much farther?"

"Not much longer." The Frost was turning into a misty gray as the shadows deepened and the sunlight darkened, screened out by the clouds. "Maybe ten minutes."

We continued on, pressing deeper and deeper. The path wove under and squeezed between massive, icicle-encrusted stones. The memories flowed around me as

225

we ran, mingling with the present. I saw flashes of my father through the trees, but it was only my imagination. Lurking at the edge of my awareness was the sensation of being watched.

Was it dark enough for Watchers to be roaming the Frost already?

Icy fear brushed my spine and twisted around my throat. I pushed the thoughts away and kept moving. At my side, Adam matched me stride for stride.

Suddenly, abruptly, a shape rose from the gloom.

The shed.

We paused together, panting, our breaths coming out in clouds of mist. The shed was just as I remembered it—small, weathered, with a sagging door and a single window of clouded glass. The trees bent over it, and their branches brushed the ice-covered roof. The path stopped at the door.

"He used to keep his traps here," I said, stepping forward. My hands shook as I reached for the knob, and my scalp prickled as the hinges whined. The elements had warped the wood, and the door groaned like a dying man as we forced it open together.

Inside, the floor of unpainted planks rattled under our feet. Light trickled through the dirty windowpane and lit the room faintly. My heart thumped hard as I brushed my fingers over the walls. Old chains and traps with their rusted teeth gaping like jaws hung from the ceiling and cast a kaleidoscope of shadows across my hands.

We stopped in the middle of the room, and the silence rushed in and wrapped us in its cold arms.

"The floor?" I said, because it was the first place that sprang to mind.

We knelt, our fingers scraping at the boards. My mittens came away grimy. Adam yanked one up. It came away in his hand without any effort revealing dirt beneath.

"That was easier than I expected," he murmured. He pulled away another board, and another.

Beneath them was a hole, and a canvas cloth. I ripped it aside, and then I froze.

A shallow pit had been dug in the dirt. The cloth had covered it. In the pit was the indention of a square.

But the device itself was missing.

"Where is it?" I gasped, tossing the canvas aside and digging into the dirt with my fingers. "Did he bury it deeper? Is this some sort of trick to deter us?"

Adam stared at the empty place, stunned. "It's gone."

We'd come all this way. We'd figured everything out. Where was it?

I jumped to my feet and dashed outside, my heart pounding and my breathing labored as I scanned the trees. Maybe my father had moved it to a new burial place. Maybe he'd hidden it behind the shed. Maybe he'd decided the floor was too obvious, or...

I lurched to a standstill as my eyes dropped to the ground. The path we'd followed through the forest was frozen dirt, but snow surrounded the edges of the shed.

227

And pressed into the pristine white of the snow…

A fresh footprint.

The blood in my veins turned to ice, and I spun for the shed. "Adam!"

He appeared in the doorway, and our gazes caught. I pointed at the print. I could barely speak the words.

"Someone has been here before us. They took it."

Adam swept the area with his gaze. He was all cold rigidity and clipped words as he turned back to me. "There're no footprints in the snow. They took the path, so we can't track them that way."

"Do you think the Blackcoats took it?"

"Who else?" he said, his eyes spitting anger. He looked at the path, and at me. "This footprint is fresh— made less than an hour ago, I'd say."

We needed to move quickly, then.

"Go," I said. "You're faster than I am. Head for the village, and I'll check the forest. They could be anywhere. But they probably haven't gotten far. Few know these woods or these paths well, but you and I do."

He nodded. "And we'll be faster if we split up. We'll meet up at the farmhouse in a few hours?"

"Yes," I said.

He took off at a run. I caught my breath and then followed, my cloak like a sail in the wind.

Snow had begun to trickle down between the treetops. A white mist enveloped the woods, turning everything gray and blue. My breath streamed from my lips and my cheeks froze as I ran.

My foot caught a root, and I stumbled. I slid off the path and landed on my knees in the underbrush. I froze at what I saw.

Footprints, veering from the path and into a snowy clearing. I saw them plainly. Adam's footprints? But no, these were smaller. They headed west, toward the lake and east of the village.

"Adam!" I screamed, hoping to call him back.

My voice was muffled by trees, the snow. Nothing responded. He was already gone.

I didn't have much time. I made the decision.

I followed the tracks.

~

My mind spun as I ran. The boards had been too easy to pull up. The thief had laid them back in place without hammering them back down. I should have immediately suspected something was amiss, but we'd been high on success. We hadn't been thinking.

Because deep down, I knew exactly who had taken the PLD, and my heart was heavy as a rock in my chest.

My lungs burned and my legs ached as I ran through the snow. I wished we'd taken the horses, but it was too late for that now. Tree branches lashed at my face and snagged my cloak, but I wrenched free and kept running.

The sunlight faded. The shadows darkened as clouds rolled across the sky. More flakes trickled down through the trees, dusting my face. The wind bit at my nose and numbed my fingers. I ran and ran and ran.

229

Finally, the gloom of the Frost gave way to the glow of light, and I broke through the tree line. Ahead, a vast lake of clouded ice stretched toward a far shore lined with pines. To the right, a tendril of white smoke from the village blacksmith curled to the sky. I was at the lake, and less than a mile from Iceliss.

The wind whipped my hair into my eyes and made them water as I scanned the shoreline. Nothing moved against the backdrop. The ice reached out over the dark water like a cloudy cataract over the iris of a black eye, and beyond the ice the river rushed past, foaming against the rocks in its path as it sped toward the falls far beyond.

I cupped both hands over my mouth and inhaled deeply, preparing to shout.

A movement at the edge of the forest farther away caught my eye.

Three figures stood at the edge of the lake. The smallest broke away and struggled through the snow toward the trees, her head bent against the wind.

I went still as a pang of certainty pierced my heart. "Ivy!"

She jerked at the sound of my voice, looking around wildly, and then her gaze settled on me. She fled into the forest.

The other figures turned.

One straightened and pinned me with a glare.

Leon.

Then I recognized the other with a jolt of shock.

Everiss.

I was torn. Ivy or the PLD? I looked after my sister, but she'd already vanished in the direction of the farm.

Everiss cradled a small case in her arms. The rusted metal cylinder gleamed in the pale light, and I sucked in a breath as I realized what it was.

The PLD.

"That's mine," I said sharply, stepping closer and stretching out one hand. "Give it back."

Leon laughed, a harsh bark in the stillness. "Finders keepers," he said, giving me a nasty smile.

"Give it to me," I repeated.

Everiss shot a glance at Leon. He shook his head, still smiling. "Maybe you shouldn't have burned your bridges. You scorned our offer, and now I'm scorning yours."

"I need it."

"Too bad," he drawled.

"You don't even know what it is," I said, desperate now.

"Neither do you."

"Please," I said, trying a new tack. "This is important. It's going to help us defeat them. You want that, too."

"The Farther nobleman wants this device," he interrupted. "And he promised to free our friends if we brought it to him."

I sucked in a frantic breath. Korr. If they gave him the PLD, it was all over. "Are you insane? Farthers don't play fair. They'll take the device and punish your friends anyway!"

"Go home, Lia Weaver," he said, his brow furrowing. "You've lost."

I looked at Everiss, but she wouldn't meet my eyes. I turned back to Leon. He smirked, triumphant.

"No," I growled. I grabbed for the case in Everiss's arms.

A knife appeared in Leon's hand. I skidded to a stop as Everiss gasped.

That was when I heard the gunshot.

NINETEEN

THE SOUND OF the gunshot rolled across the lake and reverberated through me. I threw myself into the snow. Leon staggered back as blood blossomed across his shirt, and he sank to his knees. Everiss screamed his name.

From the tree line, a figure emerged carrying a pistol.

Korr.

I couldn't move. My legs were ice, my lungs empty of air. But Everiss wasn't so afflicted. She ran, her cloak fluttering behind her like a stream of black smoke as she fled for the lake. And I watched, spellbound, as Korr lifted his arm and fired again.

"No!" I screamed.

The second sound of the gunshot shattered the silence. Everiss dropped like a bag of rocks, and the PLD flew out of her arms. It skittered across the ice and into the river.

Everiss staggered up again and stumbled into the water as red streamed down her arm. Korr rushed past me, and I thought he was going to shoot her again, but then I realized he was going for the PLD.

The case whirled as it hit the current, and rushed out of sight around the frothing curve that led to the falls. My whole being ached as I watched it disappear.

Everiss reached the other side of the water. She pulled herself out and disappeared into the woods. Korr stared for a long time at the place where the PLD had been, and then he turned and strode toward me.

My gaze slipped to the gun in his hand. Should I run? He'd already seen my face. He would only send soldiers to the house. What should I do?

Korr reached my side. He crouched down and peeled off a glove. When he felt for Leon's pulse with cold, clinical precision, my stomach lurched, but still I willed myself to look.

All the color had bled from Leon's cheeks. The snow around him was stained red. Was he dead?

Korr stood and pulled his glove back on. His eyes flicked to mine.

I couldn't stop my legs from trembling, but I didn't cower or flinch away. I would face my death with dignity.

My chest ached, and the backs of my eyes burned as I searched the far shore for any sign of Everiss. But she had vanished.

"This is a very unfortunate turn of events for both of us," Korr said. His tone was perfectly controlled, but an edge sharpened the words. He was angry, perhaps lethally so. He'd already killed one person and signed the death warrant of the other. Everiss would not last long wounded, wet, and wandering the Frost wilderness.

Dimly I became aware of footsteps, voices shouting. Farther soldiers burst from the woods, scanning the scene. The soldiers guarding the Cage must have heard the gunshots.

"Blackcoats," Korr said by way of explanation. "One got away." He pointed at Leon. "This one's dead."

Two of the soldiers picked up Leon's body as casually as if he were a sack of potatoes. The other grabbed my arm. "Shall I escort her to a detention cell, Sir?"

I couldn't breathe.

This was it.

"No," Korr said.

I blinked. Surely I'd heard him wrong.

"She isn't with the Blackcoats," Korr said crisply. "She was just looking for her sister. Let her go."

The soldier released me and stepped back. I stared at Korr. The wind caught his hair and threw it into his eyes, hiding them from me. Around us, the soldiers stomped and muttered. They took Leon's body and headed back for the village.

I didn't know what to say.

Korr's hand shot out and grabbed my wrist. He turned it over, and the bracelet glimmered in the light. I couldn't speak.

"You helped my brother," he said quietly. "Now I've helped you. We're even. Expect no other kindness from me."

His brother. Gabe. I was numb. I was frozen. I felt nothing as I absorbed the words, nothing except the knowledge that my speculation had been true...and the knowledge that it changed everything.

He was not what I'd thought he was.

"Go," Korr said sharply.

I nodded and stumbled back. He made no move to stop me. I backed toward the woods, and finally, I turned and ran.

~

I reached the farm just as the snow began to fall in earnest. White poured from the sky like a flurry of feathers, cascading over the farmhouse and blanketing the roof of the barn. I stumbled on the step and almost fell. My hands shook as I opened the door.

Jonn clawed up from his chair and took a staggering step toward me. "Lia," he gasped. "Are you—? I thought—"

I rushed to the fire and began stripping off my wet mittens and cloak. The fire was too hot, and my skin stung as it thawed. "I'm all right. Is Ivy here?"

"She's upstairs. She wouldn't tell me anything when she came home."

I lifted my aching fingers to cover my face. "She stole the PLD and took it to the Blackcoats. She must have heard us talking and slipped out this morning when we thought she was asleep. I confronted them, demanded it back, and then Korr showed up with Farther soldiers." I took one shuddering breath and let it out. "Leon is dead. Everiss too, I think."

Jonn went very still. He didn't ask for clarification, but his eyes begged me.

I told him the rest in halting sentences.

A rap at the door made my stomach jump. I rose, my heart hammering. Had soldiers come for me? Had Korr gone back on his promise?

It was Adam. He swept inside before I even reached the door to open it, his face a storm of emotion and his shoulders taut as he called out. "Has Lia—?"

He stopped, stared at me. "*Oh.*" He reached out one hand but didn't touch me, as if he feared I would break. Then he grabbed me in a tight hug. "I thought you were injured, or worse," he whispered against my hair.

"I'm all right," I said, but my words were wooden. The weight of our failure lay heavy on my chest. I didn't want to have to tell him that the PLD was lost forever.

He pulled back, rubbing a hand over his eyes as if he couldn't trust them to stay dry. "I heard the gunshots from the village." His gaze searched mine.

My stomach sank. I might as well get this over with. I looked over my shoulder at Jonn, seeking some shred of support from him as I imparted the news, but he was staring out the window. I turned back to Adam.

"Something terrible happened," I began.

"Quick," Jonn interrupted, urgently motioning to us both. "Help her!"

He'd dropped his crutches and was clutching the windowsill with both hands. I ran to his side. "Jonn?"

But my brother gestured wildly at the door. Adam crossed the room in two strides and wrenched it open. Snowflakes swirled in. I hurried to his side.

A cloaked figure staggered across the yard, falling to its knees a few feet from the porch. The snow almost completely obscured the face as it lifted, but there was no mistaking the curly hair fluttering in the wind.

"Everiss," I breathed.

She tried to speak and couldn't. Her lips were blue, her mittens missing. Her eyelids fluttered as she looked at me, and then her head sagged forward. The falling snow began to cover her shoulders and hair.

Adam stepped forward and scooped her up in his arms. She made a soft moan of pain, like a baby. Her frozen fingers clutched at his shirt, and he cradled her gently as he brought her inside and laid her by the hearth.

Jonn hobbled to her side and slumped to his knees. "Everiss?"

I ran for blankets. When I returned, Adam was peeling her wet cloak from her body.

"Please, don't let me die," she whimpered. Her eyes darted from my face to Jonn's.

"Just lie still." I snapped open a quilt and laid it in front of the fire. Adam had already gotten her out of her dress, too, and she was shivering in her shift. I dropped another blanket over her shoulders, then I handed him the rest of the blankets and grabbed the kettle to heat water. We had to work fast to keep her from freezing.

"Please," Everiss repeated, the plea as soft as a kitten's mew.

"Shhh," I said, taking her hands between mine and chaffing them. Her fingers were cold as icicles. "You'll be all right now. We'll get you warm." I paused. "Does anyone else know you're here? Did anyone follow you?"

"They think I'm dead. No one knows."

The water began to steam. Everiss's cheeks were bright red, and her eyelids drooped.

"Should we try to get her to the village tomorrow?" I asked Adam in a low voice.

"No!" Everiss's eyes flew open, and she struggled into a sitting position. "Please, let me stay here... that Farther will kill me."

I bit my lip. It was so dangerous—too dangerous. I looked at Adam. He looked at me.

She was an enemy.

"Perhaps the Blackcoats—"

"I didn't come empty-handed," Everiss interrupted. She pointed weakly at her bag, which lay with her wet clothes. "Open it."

Adam stooped and picked up the canvas sack. My heart began to beat against my ribs as he lifted something out. A long, thin cylinder wrapped in black, shiny material.

Everiss licked her lips. "I think you know what that is," she said quietly.

Adam went very still. He raised his eyes to Everiss's. "The PLD."

She nodded.

He handled it carefully, almost reverently. He popped open the metal casing and withdrew the device.

We all stared. It looked like nothing more than a collection of metal hoops the size of my palm, with a few wires to connect them and a small metal box with a switch. This was the thing we'd risked everything for? What was it? What did it do?

"How...?"

"When I heard about the Farther's proposal regarding this device, I decided to steal it for myself," Everiss said, her voice just a rasp in the silence. "I thought..." She faltered. "I thought my sister and I could use it to bargain for our father's release."

Adam and I exchanged a glance.

"Leon didn't know, but I'd already slipped it out of the outer case and put it in my bag when you burst from the woods," she continued. "When Korr showed up and shot Leon, I—I panicked. I dropped the outer case in the water and ran without thinking."

"The case is waterproof," Adam said. He ran his thumb over the material, his face thoughtful.

"Why give it to us now?" I demanded.

"I need to convince you to let me stay," she said, flushing. "We haven't always been the best of friends, and...and I know you must despise me now for siding against you with the Blackcoats. But my family doesn't have a home anymore, and even if they did I could never get past the guards anyway. I have nowhere to go but here."

It was true. She was destitute. She needed our help.

"Clever of you," I said.

Everiss's cheeks reddened. "My motives are not completely mercenary. The Farther soldiers need to be stopped. They took my father. They stole our property. They shot Leon. The list could go on and on. This device will help with that, won't it?"

"Yes," Adam said quietly, when everyone looked at him to answer. "In a way."

"Then I'm giving it to you. For justice. And—and for a place to stay." She looked at my brother.

"I don't know," I began, speaking to Adam for help. "We can't trust her. She's with the Blackcoats now—"

"Lia," Jonn snapped. He looked at Everiss, and his expression turned gentle. "It's *Everiss*. We've known her all our lives. She stays."

Shocked by his insistence, I turned and left the house. The wind bit my cheeks, and I crossed my arms to warm myself as I stared hard at the cloudy sky.

The door creaked behind me, and I turned to see Jonn hobbling out on his crutches. His face was white with pain, but he didn't stop until he was at my side. His breath came in gasps from the effort of struggling through the snow, and by the time he reached me some of my anger had cooled into simple sadness at the whole confusing situation.

"I'm sorry I upset you," I said after a pause. "I just don't trust her, and I want us to be safe."

Instead of replying, Jonn looked toward the trees. The wind made his hair flutter around his ears and across his forehead. "There are things I've never told you," he said.

I turned my head to stare at him, confused. "What?"

"When our parents were still alive, I wrote letters to various people in the village for a few years, to help with my penmanship and schooling. Do you remember? It was Da's idea. A way to keep me from descending into complete loneliness. He delivered them when he went into town with the quota each week, and brought me the replies."

"I remember," I said, and I did—faintly. "That was years ago, I thought."

"Most of them were. But one letter writer continued to write me after all the others stopped." He hesitated. "Everiss."

"What?" Astonishment skittered through me. *Everiss?*

"We were friends. Unlikely friends, yes, and she never told you because she wanted to keep it a secret. She was embarrassed, writing the poor crippled Weaver boy."

"What could Everiss possibly have to say to you?" I said, before I could help myself.

He sighed. "Don't be that way. She's smart, you know? She's witty, and observant. Most people don't know that about her."

"Anyway," he continued, "after Ma and Da died...well, it was probably best that we stopped writing letters anyway. Her parents were pushing her to become betrothed, and everything was changing. It was hardly appropriate that she continue to correspond with me, especially since I—" He stopped.

And I understood.

"I love her," he said. "I know it's stupid, but I do."

"She called off her engagement," I reminded him.

"I know. Perhaps it means something." But I could see from his expression that he wasn't hopeful. "But we have to let her stay, Lia."

This I could understand—the wild, irrational, intense need to protect and cherish. Love. It made us do the stupidest, most dangerous things.

And without it, we would wither.

"All right," I said.

~

I spent some time alone in the barn, checking the animals' food and water, making sure they were settled for the night. My mind spun with thoughts. Korr had let me go. Ivy was safe. Everiss was alive. We had the PLD.

But what happened now? Leon had been shot. Korr had been—as far as he knew—thwarted, and surely he wouldn't be happy about it. My brother had told me his deepest secret. And now we were harboring a Blackcoat fugitive.

If Raine discovered it, we'd all be killed.

The creak of the door opening alerted me. "Adam?" I called, triumphant that I'd heard him this time.

"Not Adam."

243

My stomach twisted, and suddenly I found it impossible to get a breath as I recognized the voice. *Ann?*

I turned, and there she stood, her red hood bright in the gloom, her hands clasped in front of her and her cheeks flushed from the cold.

"I had to come see you. I heard about..." She stopped.

Everiss. She'd heard that Everiss was dead. I shut my eyes and pressed my lips together as reality sunk in. She thought our friend was dead, and I couldn't tell her otherwise because it was all part of the world of secrets I now inhabited, a world she didn't share with me.

"Oh, Ann," I said, and my eyes burned with unshed emotion.

She clutched me close, and her tears dripped onto my neck. "I can't stay long," she whispered. "But I had to come see you."

"Have you seen her family?"

"Not yet. But I will. I need to make sure Jullia is all right. Maybe—maybe she can stay with us for a while. Help me with my quota."

"Is your house still standing, then?"

Ann shrugged. "Officer Raine would never let it burn down, not when he spends so much time there."

I smiled faintly.

Ann hesitated. Her hands slipped from my shoulders. "I have something else I have to tell you."

Her voice was suddenly softer, breathier.

I drew back as fresh apprehension brewed in my stomach. "Tell me what?"

It'd been a day of revelations, each one more shocking than the last. What did Ann have to say?

She pinched her lips together and looked away. "I shouldn't be telling you this. I know I shouldn't. But I have to."

I waited, nervousness rioting in my stomach.

Ann drew away and rubbed her arms. Her lips parted, and she flicked her tongue over her teeth before darting a look at me and then away. "I'm working with the Thorns," she blurted.

The words struck me like raindrops.

My breath whooshed from my lungs as shock hit me in the stomach. "What did you say?" I stammered out. I could barely speak. I stared at her, my mouth hanging open.

"I'm with the Thorns. I'm an operative." She clasped her arms across her chest as if she were cold. "I've been one since my father started taking me to Aeralis. I met someone in the city...he said I was perfect for the job...no one suspected. Not timid little Ann." She smiled sadly. "I've been passing on information ever since. And when I lured you to the village for questioning—" Her face crumpled, and she lowered her head. "I had to play along, pretend to give Korr what he wanted so he wouldn't suspect anything. He was scrutinizing me too much. I didn't want to do it, Lia. But I had to. He had to think he was winning. He had to think he'd bested me." She peered at me. "Lia?"

I was still standing there, my arms dangling. Ann, a Thorns operative. My world had just turned upside down. I shook my head, trying to make sense of it, trying to rein in the thoughts spinning like mad through my mind.

Ann took my head-shake as a signal of refusal, and her shoulders sagged. "I am sorry I couldn't tell you sooner. I...I hope someday you can forgive me."

I found my voice. "Don't be ridiculous. Forgive you? You're a hero."

Her smile was like sunshine. She grabbed me in a hug and squeezed me so tight I could barely breathe. "Now we can work together. I'm so proud of you for everything you've done. I always thought you'd be a fantastic operative."

The door creaked behind us, and we turned together. Adam.

He paused, startled to see Ann.

"I told her," she said, lifting her chin.

Adam had known, too?

Ann looked defiant, but her lips trembled. I glanced from his face to hers. Adam must be her superior, too, if she had to explain her actions to him. "I had to."

He didn't look angry. His eyes cut to mine, and his mouth softened, although he didn't quite smile. "I understand."

She turned back to me. "I have to go before it gets too dark. I'll see you in the village. Until then—be safe, Lia." Her eyes watered a little. "So many of us have been lost already."

"Wait!" I grabbed her hand, and a smile broke across my face. If she was with the Thorns, then I could tell her about Everiss. "I have one bit of good news."

TWENTY

LATER, I WENT into the village for extra supplies. We needed medicine for Everiss, and we'd need more food with an extra mouth around.

A crowd was milling around the steps to the Assembly Hall. I paused, my heart in my throat.

Officer Raine stood on the steps, flanked by soldiers.

"No member of the village may be out after dark, on pain of death. No member of the village may be found defacing Aeralian property, on pain of death. No member of the village may be found harboring enemy fugitives, on pain of death..."

I stood in shocked silence, listening, until Ann found me.

"What's going on?" I asked her.

She was quiet a moment. "Korr is furious about the loss of the device he was seeking, and he's urging a crackdown. Raine is furious about Everiss's escape. They're tightening their grip on us." She sighed. "So it begins."

"What begins?"

Ann's eyebrows pinched together as she frowned. "What we had before was nothing compared to what's going to happen now."

"What are we going to do?" I struggled to breathe. My lungs felt tight, my throat was squeezing shut. I'd never felt so trapped, so helpless. I hated it.

She squeezed my hand tight. There was nothing to say.

We stood a while longer, united in misery and hopelessness, listening as Raine read the new list of rules that would bind us into further servitude. My heart sank lower and lower.

The darkness was just beginning. I could feel it.

~

Jullia came just before dark to see her sister. She was almost swallowed by the cloak she wore, and her eyes were huge in her pale face. She knocked furtively at the door, looking all around her at the trees and snow. I answered it, stepping back to let her in.

"Thank you," she whispered, her eyes darting to my face and then away. "You've helped my family so much. How can we ever repay you?" She caught sight of her sister bundled by the hearth and let out a low cry.

"I'll be in the barn," I said, and slipped out as Jullia was dropping to her knees to embrace her sister.

Apprehension gnawed at the edges of my mind while I did the chores. I still didn't know how I felt about keeping Everiss with us. On the one hand, she needed our help and she was an old friend. But...she'd betrayed us. She'd been helping Leon steal the PLD. She'd been a part of the Blackcoats. She'd had a hand in corrupting my sister, for goodness sake.

Jonn was determined to help her, to hide her, but I felt uneasy about it. I wasn't about to turn her out into the snow, but...I wasn't exactly ecstatic about having another mouth to feed, another secret to keep. Especially a secret that might bite me back.

Another fugitive, another choice.

I thought of Gabe and my heart throbbed, but the ache was duller than before.

~

I remained in the barn, alone, until Adam found me. He'd been practically living at our house since Everiss had showed up, so I wasn't surprised to see him.

We stood in silence a few moments, him leaning against the cow pen and me stroking the nose of the horse we now called Officer Raine.

"It's been quite a day," I said finally. "I went into the village. Everything is going wrong—Raine isn't even pretending benevolence anymore. He's instituting martial law. Our autonomy, our freedom...everything is lost."

"Not everything," Adam said softly. And I knew he meant the PLD.

There was still hope, although it seemed a tenuous hope in this moment of darkness. "What will we do?" I whispered.

"We'll stick together," he said. "Help each other. Lean on each other. Bonds of love and loyalty are stronger than fear."

His voice was low and impassioned, as beautiful as music. But he looked tired. Dark shadows ringed his eyes, and his shoulders weren't as straight as usual.

Our eyes met, and warmth curled in my stomach. I remembered the palpable relief that had covered his face when he'd found out I was alive, and something in my chest loosened. I took a step toward him.

Adam tracked my movement with his eyes. He didn't move, but he looked as though he wanted to back up. I halted, reaching out to touch him. My fingers paused just before his face.

"You were worried about me," I said. "Yesterday, when you came back to the house and didn't know where I was."

A faint blush rose along his neck. "It happens," he admitted.

I bit my lip. I was still reeling from the craziness of the past few days, and I was so exhausted and emotionally drained I didn't care to analyze what I was doing. I touched the side of his face, and his eyes fluttered closed. He sighed. I stepped closer, until I felt the warmth of him rolling off his skin onto mine.

Bonds of love and loyalty...

"Adam," I whispered.

His eyes snapped open just before I could kiss him, and he grabbed my wrists and pushed me gently away. I didn't miss the ache that filled his eyes, though, and it mirrored the feeling in my chest.

"Why?" I demanded.

He sighed again, leaning forward until his forehead touched mine. "We can't," he said.

I jerked away. "Why not?"

"Lia...the PLD..."

"What? What is it? What does this device do?" Hot, sudden anger filled me. Was he going to try to invent some insulting excuse involving that snarl of wires and metal? This was going to be impressive. "Don't tell me it prevents people from kissing—"

Adam shut his eyes. "Lia, I'm trying to be a gentleman."

I could only stare at him. What was he trying to say?

"I just...I just don't think you'll want to kiss me, not after you know," he said finally. His brow furrowed, and his eyes sparked with sadness beneath his long lashes.

I just don't think you'll want to. Hurt from his rejection surged in me. "How do you figure that?" My patience was growing thin. I'd had far too many secrets revealed to me in the last few days. I didn't know if I could stand another. If he was about to tell me he'd been writing letters to some woman in Aeralis, or that he was in love with Ann...

"Lia," Adam said.

"Tell me!"

"Because we're going to get him back."

252

The ground seemed to fall away around me. My heart stuttered and then began to beat faster. "What did you say?"

Adam paced to the door and back again, his shoulders taut, his hands gripping his arms. "The PLD. I only found out days ago, and I didn't want to give you any false hope if we didn't succeed in finding it. But I got word from my superiors about the function of the device." He paused. "PLD stands for Portable Locomotion Device."

Portable Locomotion Device.

My mind spun. Sweat broke across my back. "Portable," I said aloud. I still couldn't formulate any coherent thoughts. I needed him to spell it out for me. "Locomotion?"

He looked straight into my eyes. His own were resigned, tired. "It's another gate. A working one."

My mouth dropped open as my mind spun. Things he'd said before rushed back to me, but I needed him to spell it out explicitly. I dared not hope otherwise. "And that means?"

"Those people we sent through the portal for their own safety...they were unreachable. The portal only went one way. They were safe—or lost—forever."

"And now?" My heart thundered in my chest. My mouth was dry. I couldn't draw breath.

He turned his head, as if he couldn't bear to look at me any longer.

"Now we're going to use this device to bring them back."

Book #3 in the Frost Chronicles series coming soon!! Look for it Winter of 2012/2013

Acknowledgements

Many thanks to...

My husband, Scott, for his tireless support. Thank you for being my first and last reader, and for all the hours you've spent hashing out plot points and helping me figure out character motivation. You are so wonderful, babe.

Dani, for doing a fantastic job as my editor. You rock!

Yosh, for reading the first couple chapters and offering valuable feedback.

Mom, for being an excellent beta reader.

My entire family, for constantly asking me when the next book will be finished so they can read it.

Daniel and Dru DeWitt, for being so encouraging about the progress of this book.

All my readers—thank you everyone who's written me emails, messages, or tweets expressing your love for the Frost Chronicles series or your anticipation of this book! You guys are the best. I love you all.

About the Author

Kate Avery Ellison lives in Atlanta, Georgia with her husband and two spoiled (but extremely lovable) cats. She loves dark chocolate, fairy tale retellings, and love stories with witty banter and sizzling, unspoken feelings. When she isn't working on her next book, she's reading, watching TV, or creating art.

You can find more information about Kate Avery Ellison's books and other upcoming projects online at http://thesouthernscrawl.blogspot.com/.

<u>Read the first chapter of *The Curse Girl,*
available now in paperback and ebook
format!</u>

ONE

My father drove me through the woods in his truck, the wheels shuddering over the dirt road while the air hummed with all the unspoken words between us. The tears wriggled down his wrinkled cheeks only to get lost in his beard. The mark on his wrist burned at the edge of my peripheral vision, as if it were glowing.

I sat silent and immobile, a statue, a paper doll, a frozen thing of stone.

When we reached the gate I drew one shuddering breath and let it out, and my father put his hand on my shoulder. His fingers dug into my skin.

"He promised he wouldn't hurt you, Bee. He *promised.*"

I shifted. His hand fell limply on the seat between us. He didn't try to touch me again.

Dad turned off the engine and we sat wrapped in the silence. I heard him swallow hard. I slid my fingers up and down the strap of my backpack. My mouth tasted like dust. The car smelled like old leather and fresh terror.

Nobody knew if the legends were lies, myth, or truth. But they all talked about the Beast that lived in the house. Some said he ate human children, some said he turned into a vicious creature in the night, some said he looked like a demon, with flames for eyes.

A trickle of sweat slipped down my spine.

"You don't—" My father started to say, but he hesitated. Maybe he'd been hoping I would cut him off, but I didn't. I just sat, holding my backpack, feeling the crush of responsibility slip over my shoulders and twine around my neck like a noose.

Through the gate I could see the house, watching us with windows like dead eyes. Trees pressed close to the bone-white walls like huddled hags with flowing green hair, and everything was covered with a mist of grayish moss. I'd heard the stories my whole life—we all had—but I'd never been close enough to see the cracks in the windowsills, the dead vines clinging to the roof.

Magic hung in the air like the lingering traces of a memory. I could almost taste it. Voices whispered faintly in the wind, or was that just the trees? The knot in my stomach stirred in response.

My father tried again, and this time he got the whole sentence out. "You don't have to do this."

Of course I did. Of course I must. I wasn't doing this for him. I was doing it because I had no choice. With the mark on his wrist, he was a dead man. Our whole family was doomed. He knew it and I knew it, and he was playing a game of lame pretend because he wanted to sooth his own guilt. Because he wanted to be able to look back at this moment every time it crossed his mind in the future and feel that he had offered me a way out. That he'd been willing to rescue me, but I'd refused.

Instead of responding, I opened the door and climbed out. The gravel crunched under my shoes as I stepped to the ground. I shouldered my backpack and took a deep breath.

The gate squeaked beneath my hand. I crossed the lawn and climbed the steps to the house, feeling the stone shudder beneath my shoes like the house lived and breathed. The door didn't open on its own, which I had half-expected, but when I put my hand on the knob I could feel the energy humming inside it like a heartbeat.

My father waited at the car. I looked over my shoulder and saw him standing with one hand on the door, his shoulders pulled tight like a slingshot.

All I had to do was step inside. One step inside and the mark would disappear. And I could run home. I could outsmart this house. Couldn't I? I sucked in a deep breath and rolled my shoulders.

Maybe I believed that. Maybe I didn't. Why else had I brought a backpack full of clothes, toiletries?

"Bee," my father called out, and his voice cracked. I paused, waiting for more. Maybe he really was sorry. Maybe he really didn't want me to do this...

"Bee, I just wanted to tell you how thankful your stepmother and I—"

My throat tightened. He wasn't going to stop me, was he? I shook my head, and he rubbed a hand over his face and fell silent.

When he'd come home two weeks ago at three in the morning, the sleeve of his work uniform torn, his lip bleeding, and his eyes full of fear, my stepmother had cried. Really cried—wrenching sobs that made her double over and clutch at her sides. She almost looked as if she were laughing. I'd looked at him, and I could smell the magic on him. I'd known exactly where he'd been.

And there was a tiny part of me that knew then too that I'd be the one who would pay the price for his foolishness.

All I had to do now was step across the threshold. Then the mark on his wrist would vanish, and he would be free. Everything would be okay. That was all we'd promised, right?

I pushed open the door and stepped into the house. I held my breath.

Across the lawn, my father made a sound like a sob.

Was that it? Was the mark gone?

"Daddy?" I choked out, not daring to move. "Is it—?"

"It's gone, honey!"

I started to turn, but I wasn't fast enough. The door snapped shut like the jaws of a hungry animal.

I grabbed the handle and twisted, throwing my shoulder against the heavy wood. I shrieked, wrenching the handle harder.

It was locked.

I clawed at the wood with my fingernails until they bled. I pounded with my fists.

The door didn't budge. It was strong as stone.

Through the slip of glass, I saw the headlights of my father's car flick on, and the engine revved.

He was leaving me.

slid to the floor. My sneakers squeaked against the shiny marble, my fingers slipped down the polished mahogany of the door. I didn't want to look behind me into the mouth of the house, into the darkness that was going to be my home. Or my tomb. I didn't want to think of how my father would go home and my absence would be like a ripple in the house, felt for a moment and then gone from their minds. I didn't want to think about who would miss me at school. Violet. Livia. Drew.

Drew.

Grief stuck like cement behind my eyes. I wanted to cry, but I had no tears. I never had tears. My eyes burned and my throat squeezed shut, making it hard to breathe. I crouched on the floor and put my hand over my mouth and thought of Drew's hair, his eyes, his smile.

I might never see any of those things ever again.

Terror—real terror—charged through me like a storm. It pulsed through my body, pushing at my skin, wanting to get out. Like my own soul was fighting to get free of me, like my own self couldn't stand to be trapped here at this moment. It was a surge of blinding intensity, like lightning. Then I fell, panting, my hands braced on the cool floor.

"Stop it," I said aloud. "Stop this."

I didn't have to stay here. The mark was gone and we were free and I could go home—if I could just find a way out. The idea, planted in my fear-frozen mind, cracked my terror like spring warmth.

Escape.

After all, I wasn't dead.

"Yet," I muttered, and the echo of my voice, soft and velvet, whispered back to me in the stillness. I closed my eyes tight, counted to five, and opened them. And I looked at the place that was going to be my prison.

The foyer stretched up like a bell tower. A shattered chandelier lay three feet away, crystal droplets spread like frozen tears across the marble. Light slanted into the hall through arching windows, illuminating the rest of the room and striping the broken furniture and torn books with golden sunlight. In the middle of the room, papers and quills lay scattered around on the floor. It was as if a great monster had gone into a rage and shredded the room, and then fallen into a peaceful slumber after exhausting himself.

Behind me lurked a gloomy hallway, lined with doors.

I was stuck in this house. My friends couldn't help me. Drew couldn't help me. My father wouldn't help me.

A sigh slipped through my lips as I stood to my feet.

I was alone.

Alone in the house of the Beast.